LOVE ON HOLD

Following a broken engagement, Rosa takes up a friend's offer to work on her Anglesey holiday cottage. When she meets her new neighbour, brooding Welsh farmer Gareth, a powerful mutual attraction flares between them, and she agrees to work on his upcoming barn conversion. But the rich, stylish Erin seems to have staked a claim on Gareth — and Rosa's ex-fiancé Nick is harassing her. Can Rosa and Gareth forge a relationship together — or will their pasts catch up with them and ruin everything?

Books by Dorothy Taylor
in the Linford Romance Library:

HER HEART'S DESIRE
KEEP SAFE THE PAST
THE HEART'S RETURN
LEGACY OF LOVE
CONFLICT OF THE HEART
DANGEROUS OBSESSION

DOROTHY TAYLOR

LOVE ON HOLD

Complete and Unabridged

LINFORD
Leicester

First published in Great Britain in 2014

First Linford Edition
published 2015

A catalogue record for this book is available
from the British Library.

ISBN 978–1–4448–2661–6

Published by
F. A. Thorpe (Publishing)
Anstey, Leicestershire

Set by Words & Graphics Ltd.
Anstey, Leicestershire
Printed and bound in Great Britain by
T. J. International Ltd., Padstow, Cornwall

This book is printed on acid-free paper

1

Along the road just ahead of Rosa the brightly-lit windows of a convenience store were like a welcome beacon in the darkness.

'At last!' she cheered.

The village she'd been hoping to see for the last few miles appeared deserted; but, she reckoned, on this cold and wet February evening most people would probably be home preparing dinner, not coming to the end of a six-hour drive.

Spirits raised, Rosa parked up outside the store, but just as she released her seatbelt another heavy shower began to drum upon the roof of her car.

'Not now,' she groaned, peering through the windscreen which was awash with streaming water. There was nothing else for it; she needed to make a stop here so she'd best get on with it.

She reached across to the back seat

for the waterproof Nina had suggested she'd probably need while she was there. After a little wriggling it fitted comfortably and she was able to zip it up over her tan leather jacket. With the hood pulled up and her long copper hair tucked inside, she picked up her bag and got out of the car. Straight away the wind snatched at her knee-length skirt, pressing it tightly against her legs as the rain began to soak into her black tights.

Wishing she'd worn jeans instead, she gripped the hood with both hands. Head down, and questioning her earlier enthusiasm for this trip, she ran towards the shop.

'So, straight ahead at the round-about, then second left,' she repeated a short time later to the cheerful, middle-aged assistant whose name badge read 'Carys'.

'That's right.' The woman nodded, her dark curls bobbing. 'You'll find Ty Newydd a little further down the lane. You can't miss it.' With open curiosity

2

she studied Rosa for a moment. 'Holiday, is it?' she asked. 'It's hardly holiday weather just now.'

Rosa blinked, fascinated by her soft Welsh lilt. 'No, it isn't,' she agreed, her comment reminding her she had to go back outside and face the weather. She helped herself to a plastic carrier bag and began to fill it with her purchases. 'But that's OK. It's more of a working break than a holiday. I'm decorating the cottage for friends of mine.'

Carys's face lit up. 'The Sandersons from Norfolk,' she exclaimed. 'I heard they'd bought the cottage from Gareth. Nice family . . . and good customers. Those twin girls of theirs are like two peas in a pod. They've been holidaying at the Sunrise Caravan Site just down the road for years.'

Rosa nodded and tried to look as though she was hearing all this for the first time.

Gareth? She thought for a moment while she opened her purse to pay. The name rang a bell. What was it now?

Gareth . . . Pritchard. Yes, that was it; the sheep farmer Nina and Paul had mentioned. Whatever; it hardly mattered, she doubted she'd have that much to do with him.

As Carys handed over Rosa's change her attention was taken by the shop doors sliding open again. 'Now, here's someone who might be of help,' she said. 'Evening, Erin,' she called out. 'On your way to Ty Hen, are you? This lady here was asking for directions to Ty Newydd.'

'Rosa.' She quickly told Carys her name. 'Rosa Ryan.' She glanced across the shop, curious to see who Carys was calling. A tall woman of similar age to herself — and much better-dressed for the weather, in a long waxed coat — came up to the counter.

'No, I'm not,' she said abruptly. She turned her attention to Rosa. Steel-blue eyes regarded her coldly for a moment before she glanced back at Carys. 'Gareth's out.'

'Well, thanks very much for the

directions.' Rosa broke the gathering silence. 'I'm sure I'll find it now.'

'Enjoy your stay,' Carys said, looking a bit put out by the other woman's manner. 'Say hello to Gareth for me. He hasn't been in for a few days.'

'Will do,' Rosa agreed, purely out of politeness. She wondered what the other customer's problem was. Weather probably getting her down — and who could blame her? She shivered as she stepped outside. The rain was coming down like stair rods.

Her back braced against the wind, Rosa dropped the bag of groceries behind the driver's seat and scrambled into her car. After checking that Carys's instructions tallied with Nina's, she turned on the engine. As she drove off into the night, she assured herself she would soon be settled inside with a mug of hot chocolate and the day's long drive behind her.

A short time later she groaned with apprehension as the lane she'd turned onto took a sharp curve. *Here we go again*, she thought as she began to negotiate a series of tight bends taking her down the deserted narrow lane, deciding Anglesey had a monopoly on them. The rain suddenly turned to hail. All I need now, she fretted, is to meet someone coming in the opposite direction and have to reverse back up to the top road.

Chasing away the possibility in case thinking about it made it happen, her spirits rose when out of nowhere, just ahead to her right, the pale outline of a building appeared in the gloom. Could this be it?

She slowed down to a crawl, keen to find an entrance. Hailstones continued to batter the windscreen but the wipers held up. In the few seconds of intermittent clear screen, a low wall of whitewashed stone topped by wind-tossed evergreens appeared in her headlights. As she inched forward, she just had time to make out an old wooden board, with the white, roughly-painted name 'TY' followed by 'NEW', before it was lost again to the surging branches.

'Yes!' she cried triumphantly, punching the air. She'd made it. Cautiously she turned the wheel, eased the car onto a wide dirt track and continued slowly up it. As she approached the building the hail stopped as quickly as it had begun, and the moon made a brief appearance, casting a silver glow over the wet slate roof.

She frowned at its size. Nina and Paul had certainly played down their future holiday home. From what little she could make out in the headlights' beam, it looked more like a farmhouse than a cottage. She parked head-on to a broad step leading to a solid front door. Reaching for her shoulder bag, she ferreted out the set of sturdy iron keys Nina had given her.

The hail-covered ground crunched beneath her ankle boots as Rosa got out into what was now pitch darkness. *Should have brought a torch*, she told herself, as she hitched her leather bag onto her shoulder. After a little groping she felt the straps of her overnight bag and the plastic carrier. Holding both bags over her arms, she struggled for a few moments to line up the largest of the keys against the lock. Finally she felt it slide into the keyhole, and with a little more effort was able to turn it.

As she pushed open the door, a draught of warm air was a pleasant surprise; yet an unnerving feeling of the unknown overcame her as she took a step into dark, cavernous emptiness — then something cold and wet swiftly brushed against her leg.

Rosa squealed out in fright, all strength leaving her limbs as her heart struck her ribs and she almost dropped the bags. She staggered back onto the step and was about to turn to get back into her car when a plaintive mew echoed through the darkness.

Steadying herself against the wall, she took a deep breath and exhaled thankfully. It was just a cat hiding from the storm.

Tentatively, she stepped inside again

and ran her hand along the wall until she found the light switch. Gradually her eyes adjusted to the brightness now flooding a square, stone-flagged hall. She stared at her surroundings, disbelieving of their size. For a few moments she studied the dark brown woodwork, the cream walls hung with several dusty landscapes. The hall had seen better days, but a coat of paint would soon remedy that. To her left, sitting on a turned staircase, was a small black-and-white cat, wide amber eyes set in a pretty little face staring back at her.

'Thanks for that,' she said, 'frightening me half to death. You obviously don't belong here; so like it or not, madam, you'll be going back outside before I go to bed.'

The wind gusted once more and slammed the door against her back, sending her nerves jangling again. Rosa quickly pushed the door shut with her shoulder then dropped her bags to the floor.

The cat watching her every move, she

unzipped her waterproof and shook it off, then hung it on a row of coat pegs beside the door. The two working jackets hanging there puzzled her for a moment. Paul had obviously left them behind.

Now, what had Nina told her about the layout? The specifics just wouldn't come. After the trauma she'd recently been through with Nick, her memory was on a par with that of a goldfish! Still, it was more than likely that one of the two doors at the rear of the hall led to the kitchen.

Leaving her overnight bag where it was, she picked up the plastic carrier and her shoulder bag, and made her way across two well-used, multi-coloured rag rugs which softened the effect of the grey stone. She chose the door on the right. As soon as she opened it the cat jumped off the stairs and darted in ahead of her. She frowned. It appeared to know the place.

Pale, cold moonlight shimmered dimly through a large window across from where she stood, casting shadows in the room until the racing dark clouds masked them again.

Right first time, she congratulated herself.

This time the light switch was an easy find. But as she gazed around, something began to niggle. She recalled Nina's excitement when she'd told her about the cottage with its large traditional kitchen. Again, she had underplayed it — which, Rosa considered with affection, was unlike Nina. If she didn't know any different, she would think she was in the wrong house. But how could that be? She'd seen the name on the gatepost — and the key worked.

Telling herself to stop fretting, she placed her bags on the long kitchen table and walked over to the window, eager to close the curtains against the night. Then she reached for the kettle to fill it with water. The moment she flicked it on, the cat was at her feet, weaving a figure of eight between her ankles and crying out for attention.

'Come here.' She bent down and swept her up off the floor. Holding her closely against her chest with one hand, she began to unpack her groceries with the other. 'How does a saucer of milk sound?' she asked, stroking the tiny black head and enjoying the growing warmth and vibration of the small body purring against her. 'Then maybe I can have some hot chocolate in peace.'

* * *

Angry sounds, words Rosa couldn't make sense of, became part of her dream . . . *I said, wake up, will you!* Perhaps it was because she was ignoring her friends who were telling her to wake up and face the truth about Nick: what a liar and a cheat he was!

As her eyelids fluttered, she struggled to make sense of what she thought she was seeing, as blurred confusion slowly cleared . . .

Inches away from her face the bright, intelligent eyes of a black-and-white

Border Collie stared back at her. She frowned. First the cat and now a dog. *You're still dreaming*, she told herself sleepily. She closed her eyes, then forced herself to open them again just to make sure. The dog was still sitting there, motionless as a statue.

'Who are you and what are you doing here?'

Rosa flinched at the intensity of the disembodied demand. The voice was as real as the dog. Her heart began a tattoo against her ribs as she recognised a Welsh lilt, nothing like as friendly as Carys's — and definitely male.

Rosa started to push herself up from the cushion she had rested her head against for just five minutes while her hot chocolate cooled. Her heart lurched again when she focused on a pair of denim-covered legs which seemed to go on for ever. On the other side of them, a matching collie gazed at her with the same intensity.

'Are they twins?' She said the first thing that came into her head, then

13

imagined she'd heard a small sound, a giggle, coming from somewhere beyond the sofa.

Willing herself awake, she pushed herself up and swung her legs onto the floor. Still feeling a little light-headed, she gripped the edge of the sofa with both hands, then looked up beyond the jeans and the dark green waxed jacket to meet the glowering features of a tall, broad-shouldered man staring back down at her. Rain glistened in his tousled black hair and, she acknowledged, if he wasn't scowling in such a threatening way, he'd be too attractive for his own good. Her pulse, still all over the place, now danced crazily.

'How many more times do I have to ask?' he demanded again, not quite so loudly but still impatient. 'Who are you and how did you get in?'

As his thickly-lashed eyes, so dark they appeared coal-black, locked with hers, Rosa experienced a timeless connection. It was as if they already knew each other. Confused and troubled, she blinked and the moment was gone.

She knew she had to take the upper hand so she didn't appear as terrified as she felt. She stared back at him with equal anger.

'Rosanna Ryan,' she replied with a confidence that impressed her. 'Obviously I used the key — and I might well ask you the same,' she added with a touch of sarcasm.

She inched her legs to one side as several drops of ice-cold water left the bottom of his jacket and found her feet. She bent over and slipped on her boots, then quickly got up, determined to stand her ground, even though inside she was shaking.

His eyes widened slightly and he took a step back, but it didn't help that he still stood head and shoulders above her.

She bent her head back a little more. 'Well?' she demanded. 'What are you doing here?'

His expression turned to one of disbelief. He shot a glance across the room then turned back to her. 'You're in my farmhouse asking me . . . ?'

The forcefully emphasised 'my farmhouse' made her flinch again. Their eyes locked once more, confusion meeting disbelief. It was official, she concluded; she had finally lost her mind.

'Calm down, Gareth. Can't you see you're scaring her?'

Never so glad to hear a female voice, Rosa spun round to see a dark-haired woman standing near the open doorway, her hands resting on the shoulders of two small boys, one either side of her. They, too, were dressed for the weather, and were staring at Rosa with a curiosity that matched the collies' attention.

'Why were you fast asleep?' the younger of the two asked. 'It's not even our bedtime yet.'

'Shush, Rhys.' The woman ruffled his hair affectionately before ushering the boys further into the room. 'I think there's been a mistake and this lady has got Ty Hen mixed up with Ty Newydd.'

Rosa was becoming more confused.

'But I don't understand. This is Ty Newydd. Friends of mine recently bought it: Nina and Paul Sanderson.'

Immediately, she felt the atmosphere lighten, and she shot a glance at the man again. A look of comprehension had changed his expression; and, while conscious of his dark gaze still firmly fixed in her direction, she sensed he was reining in his hostility . . . just a little.

The woman's face broke into a smile.

'That explains it, then.'

Not really, Rosa puzzled, turning her attention back to her. 'I'm Betsan,' she continued. 'This is Gareth.' Then she glanced down at the boys. 'And Owen and Rhys.'

Understanding began to dawn. So this is Gareth Pritchard and his family, she thought.

'Rosanna Ryan,' she repeated. 'But I still don't understand. I saw the name on the gatepost and it definitely said 'Ty Newydd'.'

'It's a shared entrance.' Gareth's brusque voice caught her attention. 'There's a

17 ❦

separate track on the right for the cottage that you obviously missed. You're in Ty Hen, the farmhouse. Ty Newydd is the cottage attached to it.'

Rosa's back went up. 'But the key fitted,' she insisted. 'How could that be?'

The other woman sighed.

'You said you were going to see to it last — '

'Not now, Betsan.' He dismissed her with a shortness that raised Rosa's hackles further still. She noticed a frown ripple across the woman's forehead and sensed she was about to respond, but before she could, he added, 'I'll show Miss Ryan where she should be.' He turned his attention back to Rosa, his own frown still firmly in place.

'I'll be fine,' she insisted, meeting his eyes head-on. 'Just point me in the right direction and I'll be out of your hair. I don't want to put you out any more than I already have.'

She hoped he'd sensed the hint of

sarcasm in her words. OK, it must have been a shock finding a stranger in their home, but his manner had been over the top. His wife had Rosa's sympathies: living with someone as belligerent as that must be a nightmare.

'You haven't,' he said, his manner still bordering on short. 'As I said, it's right next door.'

She reached for her jacket and shrugged it on. Another wave of tiredness washed over her and she wished she was tucked up in bed. After driving the hundreds of miles between Norfolk and Anglesey with only a few short breaks, she was beginning to feel stiff all over, her limbs felt heavy, and Gareth Pritchard was becoming more annoying by the minute.

Is he always this dour, she asked herself, *or is it just me?* She picked up her shoulder bag, then remembered the plastic carrier she'd left on the kitchen counter. She turned to Betsan with a smile and asked, 'Is it OK if I get the bag I left in your kitchen?'

19

Another small frown altered Betsan's expression. Once more, Rosa had the feeling that she was about to say something but then appeared to change her mind.

'Yes, of course,' she smiled. 'Come on through.'

Gareth Pritchard remained where he was, leaving little space for Rosa to get by, so she edged past him, her body stiffening with tension as she brushed against his arm, and followed Betsan out of the room. What did it matter if she and the miserable Mr. Pritchard rubbed each other up the wrong way? She'd be so busy during the coming weeks she doubted she'd see that much of him anyway. In fact, she'd make sure of it.

He was waiting near the front door with the two boys when she and Betsan walked back into the hall. Rosa put down her bags and reached for her waterproof, feeling a little embarrassed to see a dark patch on the hall floor where it had dripped water. She gave an involuntary shiver; it was still cold and wet to the touch. She began to pull it on but it somehow got tangled up with her jacket.

'Here, let me.'

Before she knew what was happening, Gareth had taken over, and with a few deft movements the jacket was in place. Feeling like a child who hadn't got the hang of putting on a coat, she glanced up and connected with his eyes once again.

'Thank you,' she said stiffly. She looked away, confused and annoyed that her heart had picked up speed. You're shattered, she reminded herself. And you've just had a rude awakening.

'You're welcome,' she heard him say swiftly and dismissively as he opened the front door, letting in a blast of cold air.

'Goodnight,' Betsan said. 'I hope you settle in well.' She smiled. 'After the mix-up.'

'I'm sure I shall.' Rosa returned her smile and her wishes of a good night.

She'd taken an immediate liking to the woman, and pitied her being married to such a grouch.

The grouch interrupted her thoughts with: 'There's plenty of room at the side of the cottage where you can park, but it might suit you to leave your car out front for tonight.'

'Right,' she muttered. She reached down to pick up her bags, but before she had the chance to do so, he had the carrier and her overnight bag in one hand and was offering her the shoulder bag with the other.

'Thank you . . . again,' she said, feeling dizzied by the swiftness of his actions. Was he that eager to be rid of her? Apparently so.

He produced a large rubber torch from his jacket pocket, then gestured that she should go first. Rosa stepped outside, and immediately a cold blast of wind whipped her hair in all directions — but at least the rain had stopped. She gave up trying to control it, or think of the warmth and comfort she was leaving, and hurried to her car.

Nina, Paul, she winged a silent challenge to her friends, *you said this place was heavenly.*

The farmhouse door slammed. Gareth strode past her and had disappeared inside the cottage before she'd turned the ignition key. As she manoeuvred the car, the cottage lights came on and lit the way before her.

Once inside Ty Newydd's narrow hallway, her cheeks warmed as she wondered how she could have made such a stupid mistake. Right away she could see the dimensions of the cottage were on a much smaller scale to those of the farmhouse.

She cursed her stupidity. Gareth Pritchard must think he had a right idiot on his hands.

Just like Nick.

The cruel reminder came from nowhere. *We are not going there again,* she warned herself wearily as she headed for the open door at the end of the hall. A glimpse of red quarry tiles spelled out the kitchen.

As soon as she entered the room, she noticed the darkness outside was now brightly lit by powerful lights showing a barn and a run of sheds. She turned her attention back to the kitchen, and straight away her designer's eye saw its potential. It was nowhere near as big as the one she'd just left, but still a good size.

'I've turned on the water for you,' Gareth explained. He was crouched over by the sink unit with his back to her. When he got to his feet and faced her, his presence filled the room.

She sensed urgency about him, a need to be gone, but who could blame him? She'd upset his and his family's evening, and right now what he wanted, she guessed, was to see the back of her.

'Thank you,' she said. Then she felt the need to apologise. 'Sorry I got it wrong.'

He shrugged. 'A bad night, the same keys for both houses . . . easily done.' To her surprise, he had the good grace to almost look apologetic. 'I should have remembered to tell Paul and Nina about the keys; given them the opportunity to change the locks. Perhaps you could mention it and see what they want to do — although I'm quite happy to let things stand as they are.'

Rosa was somewhat taken aback by his change of attitude — and found she welcomed it.

'Yes, of course. I promised I'd ring once I'd arrived. Nina will think it hilarious when I tell her what happened. She'll say only I could have mistaken a farmhouse for a cottage.'

Was that the beginnings of a smile? Maybe; she wasn't sure, but his manner wasn't quite so brittle now. She began to relax.

'You're obviously good friends,' he said.

'We met at primary school, when we discovered we were related in a distant way. I expect you get a lot of that here on the island. When I called into the village store, Carys seemed to know all about you selling the cottage.'

He nodded and gave her a wry look. 'There's very little she doesn't know. It's a way of village life, but sometimes . . . ' He raised his shoulders.

'A bit too intrusive,' she finished, almost to herself but loud enough for him to hear and wonder what was behind the sudden shadowing of her eyes. He'd never seen such a shade before: sea-green with flecks of gold, and a fine, darker green band encircling her irises. As for her spectacular shock of red hair . . .

Swiftly, he turned his mind back to business.

'So, as I said, the water's on and I've switched on the fridge-freezer for you.' He nodded towards the corner end of the sink unit where the gleaming new appliance stood. It wouldn't do to spend time thinking about the initial impact she'd had on him when he'd found her asleep in the living room. He had a farm to resurrect and no way could he afford distractions, particularly in the form of Rosanna Ryan.

'The boiler for the heating and hot water is just here.' He walked over to where a pristine white boiler had been fitted in a recess near to the back door and opened a narrow chrome flap at the base. 'These are the controls,' he explained.

She moved over and stood beside him to take a closer look, more aware of his presence than of what he was showing her. *This isn't right*, a small voice warned. *He's a married man with children.* She tuned in again to what he was saying.

'They're very easy to use,' he added. He pressed a small button, and when a green light came on she heard the boiler fire. 'Off-switch is just alongside.' He indicated it. 'It's already pro-grammed to come on in the morning and go off again at night, and you can control the temperature by the thermo-stat in the hall.'

She nodded her understanding.

'Thanks. It all looks very straight-forward. Just one last thing,' she said. She glanced back across the room. 'Can the range be used . . . just for a fire, I mean.' In contrast to the new kitchen fittings, an old-fashioned cast-iron range and a Welsh dresser were still in place. Whether it worked or not, she hoped Nina and Paul would keep it. It added so much to the ambience of the room.

'Yes, and the oven works. Betsan baked some bread in it as a test.'

Rosa was impressed. 'Wow. Your wife must be very talented.'

A frown furrowed his brow. 'Betsan is my sister,' he said, 'not my wife.'

'Oh, I see.' For some reason, Rosa's heart sped up and she found it hard to hold his gaze.

'I'll leave you to it,' she heard him say.

'Yes, of course. I must let Nina know I've arrived.' Her eyes made a brief connection with his. 'And thanks again for all your help,' she said as she followed him down the hall.

Gareth acknowledged this with a curt nod before opening the front door. '*Nos da*, Ms. Ryan,' he said. 'It means 'goodnight' around here,' he explained when he noticed her confusion.

With that he was gone, leaving Rosa feeling slightly bewildered.

2

Waking from a deep sleep, at first Rosa couldn't place where she was — then everything came flooding back. Yesterday's journey, her first impression of the island . . . cold, wet . . .

Gareth Pritchard.

Her heart quickened as his image filled her thoughts, and the memory of his handsome craggy looks and fascinating eyes returned.

'Go away,' she murmured; but his tall, dark-haired image remained startlingly detailed in her mind. She wondered if he was as abrupt with everyone as he had been with her. She gave herself a mental shake. Right now she had her work cut out making her own life worth living.

Pushing herself up, she swung her legs out of bed. The room felt luxuriously warm. As she relished the comfort, she silently praised Nina and Paul for making central heating a priority.

Her phone lay on a straight-backed wooden chair she'd discovered the night before in the smaller of the two living-rooms; it worked well as a temporary bedside table. The time on her phone screen came as a total surprise. After what had become a routine of disturbed nights and early risings, on her first night here she'd slept through far longer than she'd expected. Maybe Anglesey was the change of scene she needed after all.

Her good mood plummeted, how-ever, when she saw there was yet another voicemail from Nick. She sighed wearily, in two minds whether to open or just delete it; but if it was something to do with the business . . . She decided to check it, but all she heard was the familiar cry she'd been hearing for the past few weeks, admitting he'd been a fool and they must talk.

31

'Oh, no, we mustn't,' she said aloud, and with feeling promptly deleted the message.

Rosa turned her mind to what she was here for. Notes and sketches on paper were fine, but now she was here, she would gain a true feel for the cottage and maybe make a few changes before she began the work.

She got up and crossed the room to take a look outside. The heavy floral curtains covering the sash windows gave no hint as to what sort of day it was. With some trepidation, she pulled both curtains aside, looked out, and blinked against bright sunlight. Before her the rolling landscape was like something out of a travel brochure. In contrast to the misery of yesterday's wind and rain, it became almost painful to gaze for too long at the vivid blue sky and the slowly drifting cotton-wool clouds high above.

Eager to see more, Rosa unlocked the window catch and pushed up the lower frame, ready to lean outside for a further look around; but the rush of cold morning air against her pale green satin pyjamas had her quickly drawing it back down again.

Rubbing her arms, she stood for a while, taking in what appeared to be the hedged boundaries of the farm. She noticed the track branching off from the lane to the cottage, which Gareth had mentioned the night before. Beyond the high-banked hedges, lush green fields rolled away to the horizon; most filled with innumerable grazing sheep, a few with newborn lambs close to their sides.

Far over to her right, beyond a ruined chapel, the land descended with a graceful sweep towards a deserted crescent beach; contrasting light and dark sand showing where the tide had reached and turned again.

'You jammy pair,' Rosa murmured; now she could understand why Nina and Paul raved about this place.

Eager to begin her day, she opened the suitcase she'd realised she needed after Gareth had left, and had quickly retrieved from her car.

Mindful of the outside temperature, she trawled through her clothes until she'd found a pair of thick brown cords, a long-sleeved cream T-shirt and a chunky blue sweater, before heading for the bathroom to shower.

★　★　★

'*Bore da*, Ms. Ryan.'

Rosa almost jumped out of her skin as the greeting came from somewhere behind her. She knew straight away it was Gareth; she would recognise his voice anywhere. She put down the box she was just about to lift out of the boot of her car and straightened up. Tucking her hair behind her ears, she turned to see him walking in her direction.

The sight of his powerful figure was more welcoming than she'd ever admit, and the quickening of her heart both disturbed and irked her. She took in his appearance as he covered the space between them. His blue check shirt was just visible beneath a thick navy sweater, and his dark work trousers were tucked into heavy-duty green wellington boots. As he came up to her he smelled of fresh air.

'Let me guess,' she said, getting back on track. 'That's Welsh for 'good morning' — and please call me Rosa.'

He looked both surprised and pleased by what she'd just said. 'Right first time . . . Rosa,' he said. 'And it's Gareth.' He offered his hand and after a moment's hesitation, she took it.

When he smiled his face was transformed. His healthy complexion, the crinkles at the corners of his black-lashed eyes and the few flecks of grey at his temples appeared accentuated by the brightness of the day. *He should do that more often*, she thought.

'You're a fast learner.'

She shrugged, still conscious of the lingering warmth of his hand, and how strong a grip he had. 'It's not too hard to figure out. *Nos da* when you left last night and *Bore da* this morning.'

'I'm still impressed.' Friendliness remained in his expression.

'I'll take that as a compliment.' She had the feeling Gareth Pritchard was not easily impressed. 'About last night, though,' she added, 'I'm sorry about the mix-up. It must have been a shock finding me flat out on your sofa.'

A shock, yes, he agreed silently; but a mesmerising one he still hadn't recovered from.

'You could say that. Sorry I bit your head off.'

'Well, I was guilty of breaking and entering.'

'Entering, yes; but as far as I can tell, you didn't break anything, did you?' His eyes twinkled. 'So I shan't be contacting the police.'

It lifted her spirits to realise they shared the same sense of humour. 'Pleased to hear it,' she said. 'That would have held up my work.'

'Work?' He appeared puzzled. 'I thought you were here on holiday.'

She shook her head. 'That would be

nice, but no, actually. I'm here to decorate the cottage. It's what I do for a living.' A small frown wrinkled her brow. 'I had — *have*,' she corrected swiftly, 'my own business.'

Gareth noticed a subtle change in her manner and a slight hesitation, as though she was considering what to say next. He wondered why.

Noticing his eyes narrow for a second, Rosa looked away. Had he picked up on her caution? It was past history — or at least it soon would be — and she didn't want him knowing any more about it.

Why is that? a small voice asked. She was not the guilty party, after all. She straightened her back and stood tall.

'I'm giving it a makeover for Nina and Paul, and,' she glanced again at the surrounding countryside, 'if there's time, I'll do a little exploring before I go home.'

As he looked at Rosa's pale face, Gareth sensed the same shadow he'd noticed in her eyes the night before, the same worrying of her bottom lip. Something was troubling her, and he suddenly wanted to know what it was, but there was no way he could ask outright.

'Makes sense, you being here this time of year other than for a holiday,' he said instead. 'The weather will get better before you leave.'

As though reinforcing his words, from somewhere close by a blackbird burst into song.

Her mood lifted. 'I'll hold you to that,' she half-joked, still slightly wary of him. She glanced around. 'I just can't believe this countryside. It's breath-taking. I've seen dozens of Nina and Paul's holiday snaps over the years but nothing of here.'

He followed her gaze as she looked beyond the quilted fields towards the impressive coastline. 'You're very lucky to live here,' she murmured.

Their eyes met again; it seemed time slowed.

'I am,' he said. 'Although I think you tend not to appreciate what you've got when it's always been there.'

She held his gaze with a smile. 'In that case you'll have to take some time out, too; look at it all through different eyes.'

No, she groaned silently. *What did I just say?* It sounded like she was suggesting they do something together, which was the last thing she'd meant. However, if he had thought the same, he didn't show it. Instead, he shook his head.

'The lambs will be coming thick and fast soon, so I'll be at full stretch with the ewes.'

She glanced away towards the fields.

'There's an awful lot of sheep out there. Do you manage all this alone?'

'Yes and no,' he said. 'In this business we tend to help each other out when needed. I've a young lad, Ifan, working for me at the moment, but he's off to college in September.'

Their conversation was interrupted

by the sudden roar of an engine and the appearance of a silver Range Rover racing up the track to the farmhouse, at a speed Rosa considered well over the top, before it came to a sudden halt in front of the farmhouse. She noticed Gareth frown.

When the driver got out, she immediately recognised the woman who'd come into the store the night before. As she turned in their direction, the movement tossed her neat blonde fringe, which swiftly fell back into place. Her stylish cherry-red coat and black leather boots made Rosa feel decidedly underdressed in her old cords and sweater.

As she came up to them, she threw Rosa a withering glance.

'Where's the fire?' Gareth teased. Met by an even darker look, he cleared his throat and began to introduce the two women. 'Rosa, this is Erin Martin. We've known each other a long time.' Rosa noticed this produced an arched eyebrow from Erin. 'Erin . . . Rosanna

Ryan. Rosa's here to decorate Ty Newydd.'

'Is that right?' She couldn't have looked less impressed. Nor did she give any indication of seeing her in the store. Rosa was then dismissed when Erin promptly looked away to give Gareth her full attention.

'Gareth, I need to — '

Whatever Erin needed, Rosa would never know, for she was interrupted by the appearance of a wiry, red-headed teenager hurrying around the far end of the farmhouse. He stopped short, looking slightly awkward when he saw all three adults looking back at him.

'Gareth,' he called, 'I think there's something happening with one of the ewes.'

Rosa guessed this was Ifan.

'Be right with you,' Gareth called back. 'Probably one of the young ewes delivering for the first time,' he said to Rosa. Then he shot a look at Erin. 'Can it wait, or do you want to come round to the sheds?'

With that he strode off in Ifan's direction, leaving Erin to stare after him with a thunderous look. The look was still firmly in place when she briefly glanced back at Rosa before she stormed off after him.

What is her problem? Rosa wondered. *How could she be such a misery on this beautiful day?*

Turning her attention to her own concerns, Rosa reached back into her car for the last box stored inside.

Yet moments later, as she placed the box on the kitchen table, she couldn't help but wonder about Gareth and Erin's relationship. He had implied they were old friends; yet Erin, she sensed, believed it was much more than that.

Ready for a coffee, Rosa had walked over to the sink to fill the kettle when her attention was caught by the sight of them standing outside a run of sheds which partly filled the length of the long farmyard. They were deep in conversation. Gareth now appeared more relaxed and there was something about Erin's body language, the way she was smiling at him and touching his arm, that spelled out a certain intimacy.

I guess I'm right, Rosa mused. The thought had no sooner formed than Gareth glanced across the yard, gesturing towards the cottage as he carried on talking. Erin looked over, too.

Straight away, Rosa could see her stony expression had returned. Despite the distance, and the fact she was partly obscured by the old-fashioned net runner stretching the width of the window, Rosa sensed Gareth's eyes lock with hers. She quickly turned away and walked over to the cupboard to take out the jar of instant coffee she'd bought at the store.

A short time later, with a steaming mug in front of her, she settled down at the table and attempted to study her sketch pad. Her concentration was everywhere but on her work as unwanted thoughts of Gareth and Erin kept popping up. It irritated her. Why should she speculate about them as a couple anyway?

She was there to do a job, not spend her time wondering about other people's lives.

She got to her feet, picked up her pad, pencils and mug, and left the kitchen. It was time to get on with what she was here for. Moments later, she heard the roar of Erin's car racing off again.

Rosa re-checked the list of materials she needed and wondered if Gareth knew of a local decorating supplier. Perhaps not; from what she'd seen of the farmhouse, it had been quite some time since anyone had taken a paint-brush to it. Still, there was no harm in asking, and it might save her trawling through the phone book.

She got up from the table and glanced outside. Apart from the two collies basking in the sunshine, the yard appeared deserted.

Despite its slight air of neglect, the size of the farm — with its huge span of concrete yard separating the farmhouse and cottage from the main barns and outbuildings — surprised her. She noticed an older and much more substantial barn some distance away from the main working area; its dark granite construction and stone staircase built into one side gave it a timeless air of permanence. *Perfect for conversion*, was the first thought that came into her head — and large enough for two separate dwellings.

A sudden bleating chorus from the other side of the yard grabbed her attention. In an open-ended barn she could just make out Gareth and Ifan: sleeves pushed up, Gareth was firmly holding a ewe while the boy watched intently. He appeared to be encouraging Ifan to take hold of the animal; which, after something of a struggle, he managed to do. Moments later, Gareth said something, and Ifan let it go.

Just as she decided to take the opportunity to go and ask him about a supplier, her mobile rang. She tensed as she picked it up. Nick's number appeared on the screen. She swiftly switched it to voicemail, a slight tremor shaking her hand.

How long is this going to go on? she fumed internally. When would he finally get the message there was nothing left to discuss — either privately or professionally? She sighed. Much more of it and she would have to change her number.

Pushing her worries to one side, she left the phone on the table and went outside. The moment she stepped into the yard, she noticed the dogs' ears prick up. As she got closer they jumped to their feet and began to bark. She stopped in her tracks just as Gareth looked over and saw her. He swiftly said a few words to the dogs, and immediately they stopped barking and sat down.

'Don't worry about Bryn and Floss,' he called to her, but as she made her way towards him she still remained a little wary.

By the time she reached the barn, he had hold of another ewe. She watched

46

as he handled the animal with ease, aware of the rippling of his muscles beneath the curling dark hair of his forearms. She listened with interest while he discussed the ewe's condition with Ifan, then released it. In seconds, it was on its feet and skittering across the straw-strewn floor to join several others huddled together in a far corner, all bleating in full chorus.

He threw her a smile. 'Won't keep you,' he said over the noise before reaching for a bar of soap set next to a bucket of water. He washed his hands, then dried them on a towel hanging from a nail. As he rolled down his shirt-sleeves, he said something to the dogs in Welsh which set their tails sweeping the floor. 'Stroke them if you like,' he encouraged. 'They won't harm you.'

A little tentatively, she did as he suggested; and soon they were vying for her attention and she was laughing at their efforts.

'They're gorgeous,' she exclaimed. 'I

can't believe how well-trained they are.'

He looked amused. 'They're working dogs,' he said. 'They soon get to know who's in charge.'

She felt she'd said something stupid. 'Of course they are.'

'D'you need help with something?'

'It's just a query. It won't take a minute, but if you're busy . . . '

'That's OK. We're finished here for now.' He nodded over in the animals' direction. 'It's looking like those ones are breech presentations. It will be good experience for Ifan to help with the deliveries.'

'Oh, I see.' She glanced over at the ewes, which had finally quietened down. 'I didn't realise that could happen with animals.'

His small smile told her there was a lot more to sheep farming than most people knew about. He turned to the boy. 'Ifan, this is Miss Ryan. The lady I mentioned who is staying in Ty Newydd for a while.'

With Gareth's formal introduction

making her feel about a hundred, she gave Ifan a broad smile and was touched to see his freckled face flood with colour.

'Hi, Ifan, I'm Rosa,' she said, wanting to put him at his ease. 'It's nice to meet you.'

'You, too,' he mumbled. Then he reached for the soap and concentrated on washing his hands.

With practised ease Gareth stepped over the metal barrier that kept the ewes contained.

'So what's the problem?' he asked.

'It's not a problem, as such,' she hastened. 'I just wondered if you knew the best place to buy paint. I want to get started as soon as possible.'

'Dafydd Hughes is your man,' he said without hesitation. 'Long-time friend of my father's. His shop's in Llangefni, but if you'd rather use those big DIY stores, there are a few on the island.'

She shook her head. 'No, I know only too well how every customer counts for small businesses. Besides, I expect he'd be able to order in supplies for me if he hasn't got exactly what I want today.'

Gareth nodded. 'I'm pretty sure he'd do that.'

'Oh, and I'll also need to hire a sander at some point. The floorboards are in really good condition, and it would be a shame to cover them with carpet or laminate flooring, but I'll need to do some sanding before I varnish them. Is there a local tool hire firm where I could get one?'

As he watched her become more animated about her work, his own interest began to grow. Would a sander take much handling? He couldn't imagine someone as fine-boned and — to put it bluntly — as skinny as Rosa wielding any sort of heavy equipment.

He mentioned a nationwide firm. 'They're in Llangefni, too. You should be able to hire one from them.'

'That's great.' Her eyes sparkled. She was keen now to get going. 'Could you give me directions how to get there?'

He checked his watch. 'I'm going

into town myself soon. I could take you if you're ready to go. I've just got to shower and change, so say . . . in about twenty minutes?'

Rosa was surprised by his offer but happy to accept it. A lift was bound to save her some time.

'Twenty minutes it is,' she smiled.

'I'll be in the Land Rover,' he said. He nodded across to the red and cream vehicle parked a few metres away next to a tractor.

'Right . . . thanks. I'll see you then.'

While she made her way back across the yard, he remained where he was, watching until she disappeared inside the cottage. There was no getting away from it, this woman intrigued him. The more he saw of her, the more he wanted to know. She was going to be here until Easter, but that was less than six weeks away. Would it be long enough? Suddenly time mattered.

'Gareth, will the ewes stay in the barn for now or should I put them in the sheds with the others?' Ifan asked, breaking into Gareth's reverie and making him blink.

* * *

It really is a different world, Rosa thought, as Gareth drove confidently at speed up the twisting lane she had literally crept down the night before. The tall banks on either side were alight with drifts of pale yellow primroses, and here and there fat clumps of daffodils were poised ready to burst into flower. Everything looked so fresh, so alive, and sparkling with a remembrance of last night's rain.

When they eventually turned onto the top road and she saw for the first time the distant, snow-capped Snowdon range in sharp relief against the clear blue sky, she gasped.

He shot her a look. 'Is something wrong?'

She shook her head. 'No, quite the opposite. I never imagined it was so beautiful. No wonder Nina and Paul have fallen in love with it all.'

His mouth curved as he glanced at her again. 'I've heard it can have that effect.'

She smiled back at him. He looked striking in a fine-knit olive sweater, the crew neck showing just a hint of his check shirt collar.

As they sped along, Rosa became aware of a growing sense of wellbeing. In her heart she knew she had surfaced from the dark, despairing place she had found herself in at the start of the year. But how long would it take for the battering of her self-confidence to heal completely?

As the miles slipped by she began to draw strength from the beauty of the rolling fields, the occasional cottage; even the stark formation of copses and woodland held a particular symmetry as they awaited the first stirrings of spring.

Realising Gareth had just said something, she took control of her feelings and turned to look at him. 'Sorry,' she said, 'I was miles away.'

'I just wondered if you were still enjoying the passing scenery.'

'I am,' she said.

He looked pleased. 'I'll take you round to Dafydd's first. What I have to do shouldn't take long, then I'll come back for you.'

'You're being such a help,' she said. 'I really appreciate it.'

'No problem.' He shrugged casually. 'Like I said, I had to come in anyway.'

Rosa turned her attention back to her surroundings, but her interest was suddenly interrupted by the ringing of her phone. Her stomach flipped as she remembered the last caller had been Nick. Surely it wasn't him again — but she knew she had to check. Not recognising the number, and thinking it might possibly be potential business, she announced herself.

'Don't hang up, Rosa . . . please.' She froze, and Nick quickly took advantage of her silence. 'I've been trying to get hold of you all week. I thought I'd see you around town. Everyone I asked either said they haven't seen you or were a bit tight-lipped. Look, Kirsty and I are having problems . . . '

Rosa's eyes widened. She couldn't believe his gall! 'And why should that concern me?' she asked coldly.

'She says it's all the stress I'm putting her through over having to close the business. I'm sure you and I could work through all that's happened and keep it running. It makes sense for you as well as us. She says she wouldn't mind. It's crazy to dissolve the partnership when the company is doing so well.'

Rosa felt nauseated. She couldn't believe the utter nerve of him — Kirsty wouldn't mind! What about her feelings — not to mention the small matter of Kirsty's pregnancy? He must either be a fool or his ego had grown out of all proportion.

'Darling . . . ' His voice softened. ' . . . just think about it. We were a great team once, weren't we? It would be a financial disaster for us both to let it all go. Can't we meet up, talk it over? I'm sure you'd feel differently face-to-face.'

'That is never going to happen,' she replied through gritted teeth. 'I can't believe you could even think it, let alone have the nerve to suggest it.'

'Well, that's just typical of you!' His tone changed dramatically. 'If that's the way you feel,' he snarled, 'don't think it's going to be all plain sailing. I'll catch up with you one way or another, and when I do, you'll — '

'If you contact me again, I'll be the one to take it further,' she cut in swiftly, his veiled threats scaring her. With shaking fingers and a thudding heart, she disconnected the call, switched off her phone and threw it back into her bag as though it was contaminated. Feeling the strength had been wrenched from her body, she leaned back in her seat and closed her eyes, willing her heart to slow down.

Nick had obviously bought a pre-paid phone, she fretted, knowing she wouldn't recognise the number; that was typical of the devious behaviour she'd come to recognise towards the end of their relationship. One thing for sure, she fumed silently, he wouldn't catch her out again.

Aware she had ended the call, Gareth shot her a glance, and her ashen colour and strained features shocked him. He quickly pulled the vehicle over into a gated entrance to a field.

'Rosa,' he began cautiously, 'are you OK? I couldn't help but overhear . . . is someone harassing you?'

She opened her eyes and for a moment stared ahead, registering nothing as she tried to gather her thoughts. When she finally looked at him, the concern she met in his expression made her swallow hard and she tried to pull herself together. 'It was nothing . . . really,' she began, a little shakily. 'Just a bit of a shock. It was the last person I expected to hear when I answered.'

'Right,' he said slowly, wondering what to say next. From his frown, she knew this wasn't much of an answer, and felt he deserved more.

'It was my ex-fiancé; we're still in the process of tying up some loose ends. We were business partners as well as . . .'

'Oh, I see.'

She glanced away again, and although he felt it would do her good to get it off her chest, he sensed that was all she was willing to say.

'Still feel like shopping for paint?' he asked, once the colour had returned to her cheeks.

His tentative smile, which she read as an attempt to raise her spirits, touched her. Despite her promise to herself that it would be a long time, if ever, before she succumbed to the attractiveness of a man again, she felt comforted.

Digging deep, she found her sense of humour. 'Well, I'd rather shop for shoes, but as I'm here to work, paint has to stay at the top of the list.'

'Dafydd's it is, then,' he said, pleased to see she'd brightened. He switched on the engine and turned back onto the road.

Deep inside, still not over the shock of Nick's call and what he'd ended up saying, Rosa was still trying to push all thoughts of him away as they entered the town of Llangefni. She glanced with interest at the variety of small shops set either side of the narrow one-way street Gareth had taken, which ended at the town square with a river running alongside it.

'This is it,' he said moments later as they pulled up outside a double-fronted shop.

'What about the dogs?' she asked, after they'd climbed out of the Land Rover. She glanced in the back of the vehicle where Bryn and Floss had been sitting since they left the farm. Now they were on all fours looking expectantly at Gareth.

'They'll be fine here.' He said a few words and they settled down again.

As he ushered her inside the shop the tinny sound of an old brass bell announced their arrival. She was pleased to see it was well-stocked. A short, grey-haired man stood bent over some paperwork at the far end of a long, well-worn counter. He glanced up and, seeing Gareth, his face broke into a huge smile.

'Gareth-bach,' he greeted him. Then he beamed at Rosa, curiosity in his grey eyes.

She was then left wondering what was being said as the others conversed briefly in Welsh. From Gareth's body language she sensed he was contradicting something the other man had said — that it had been about her.

He swiftly reverted back to English to make the introductions. 'Rosa, this is Dafydd.'

'Pleased to meet you.' Dafydd offered his hand and gave hers a firm shake.

'Rosa is from Norfolk,' Gareth explained. 'She's here to decorate Ty Newydd.'

'Well, Gareth's brought you to the right place,' he enthused. 'What about some colour cards?'

'Yes please,' she smiled. 'I've a fair idea of what I want. I just need to check 'what shades you have available.'

He lifted up the counter flap. 'There's a spinner-ful over here.'

Gareth touched her arm lightly. 'I'll leave you to it,' he said. 'I shouldn't be long.'

As she glanced up and was captured by his eyes, unexpected, unwanted sensations began to stir. Shocked by the strength of her feelings, she said, more sharply than she'd intended, 'Don't hurry back on my account.'

A frown immediately ridged his brow. 'Right.' He gave her a brief nod then called out, 'See you later,' to Dafydd and left the shop.

Biting her lip, she watched him go.

'I heard Gareth had sold the cottage,' Dafydd said, breaking into her thoughts. 'You've picked one of the best spots on the island. I've always envied Owen's place.'

Rosa took this to mean Gareth's father.

'I wish.' She rolled her eyes. 'It belongs to friends of mine. I'm just the hired hand.' Still angry with herself for taking her insecurities out on Gareth, she began to choose several colour cards.

* * *

Deep in thought, Gareth strode across the town square. Why the sudden change in Rosa's attitude? She'd appeared to have got over her upset from the phone call, but now she'd gone all formal on him. His frown returned. There was no getting away from it; women were a complete mystery . . . well, some more than others. Erin, he could read like a book: one with very few pages, he grimly concluded. Betsan didn't count since she was his sister. And the girls he'd dated in the past? Well, that all seemed so long ago. He couldn't remember one half of them since he'd inherited the farm.

And now Rosa had come into his life and he couldn't get her out of his mind. After the initial shock of discovering her in his home he'd found himself utterly drawn to her, but what had he done? Gone completely the wrong way about it, that's what.

Maybe it was something to do with the row he'd had with Erin earlier that day, but it still confounded him why he'd gone straight on the defensive instead of carefully bringing her out of the deep sleep she was obviously in. Met by his tirade he'd been lucky she hadn't screamed the house down.

He reached the entrance to his bank and walked inside. 'Gareth Pritchard for Mr. Davies,' he said to the young man behind the reception desk.

'Morning, Mr. Pritchard,' he greeted him pleasantly. 'I'll just ring through for you. Please take a seat.'

Gareth chose one of the two armchairs across from the desk and sank back into the crimson upholstery. Rather than going over in his mind how he'd planned to sell his ideas for the old barn, with the hope of increasing his bank loan to finance it, his thoughts remained firmly on Rosa . . . not only was she getting under his skin, but he couldn't — didn't want to — fight the feeling.

★　★　★

'Right, let's see what the damage is.'

As Dafydd set to with a calculator, Rosa frowned at the amount of paint she'd bought, and worried about the dogs once it was all packed into the back of the Land Rover. She'd have to make some gesture of thanks to Gareth for bringing her here — but what? She baulked at offering payment, instinctively knowing he would take offence.

Dafydd broke into her thoughts with the amount she owed.

'Can I pay by card?' she asked.

'Of course.' He reached for the electronic reader and passed it to her.

'Thanks, Mr. Hughes. I wasn't expecting to get everything I needed today.'

'Dafydd, please,' he said warmly. 'We don't stand on ceremony here, especially as you're a friend of Gareth's.'

Friend? Rosa considered his assumption. Early days for it, but 'friend' suited her fine. Then she mocked herself. If impressions were anything to go by, Erin had her claws so firmly fixed into him that friendship, even a brief one, looked like being right out of the question.

So why this feeling of disappointment?

* * *

'I'm hardly going to stand by and watch you carry it in all by yourself, now am I?' Gareth said when they returned to the farm and Rosa told him she would unload the paint.

'But I've taken up enough of your time,' she protested. 'You could be getting on with something else.'

He gave her a determined look. 'It will take all of five minutes.'

She admitted defeat, found the key to the front door and opened it. 'Lined up here to one side of the hall will be fine,' she said when she turned to see him standing behind her, holding four paint cans and waiting to follow her in.

'Can I offer you a coffee?' she asked, after he had carried in more than his fair share and the job was done in the time he'd said. 'You must be ready for one by now.'

He shook his head. 'Another time perhaps; I need to catch up with Ifan.' He made his way towards the front door.

'Of course,' she hastily replied, following after him. 'Thanks again,' she said as he began to walk away. 'You've done me a huge favour.'

'Any time,' he responded casually. 'Good luck with the decorating.'

'Come and take a look if you like . . . whenever it suits you,' she called as, with a wave of one hand, he climbed back into the Land Rover and fired the engine.

And why shouldn't I invite him to? she argued with herself as she closed the front door. He had gone out of his way to be helpful; he had a history with the cottage; and, yes, she would like him to see her ideas come to life. Nothing wrong with that, was there?

Rosa picked out a can of white emulsion from the pile, carried it upstairs to what would be the twins' bedroom, then decided to carry more upstairs, too.

Some time later, eager to make a start on the ceiling in Chloe and Eva's room just to feel she had achieved something, she was just imagining how different it would look with fresh paint and girly furnishings when her mobile rang.

Her heart skipped a beat. *It can't be him again, surely,* she told herself. Reluctantly she picked it up then expelled a breath of relief when she saw Nina's number on the screen.

'Nina!' she greeted her happily. 'You must be psychic. I'm standing in the girls' room right now, thinking about the changes I'm going to make. I'm planning on making a start after lunch. I'll have to make it pretty special to fit in with the surroundings,' she chatted on. 'Why didn't you tell me this is such a breathtaking place?'

'I think I did . . . several times,' Nina said dryly. 'But what's all this about lunch? It's gone three. I've just picked them up from school.'

Rosa frowned and checked her watch; so it had.

'Tell me you had a late breakfast.'

'I did,' she agreed vaguely. She knew she'd be in for a lecture if Nina knew she'd had just one slice of toast with a cup of tea, and only coffee since. 'And the best night's sleep in ages,' she added. 'It's a beautiful day here. All this sunshine gives me the urge to get down to work.'

'Good. Now, let's talk food,' Nina said firmly.

'I'll have something in a minute, promise.'

'Well, make sure you do. I know your appetite hasn't been much of a priority for a while, but here was I thinking we'd made good progress. You can't go on picking like a sparrow. You'll make yourself ill.'

'I have made good progress,' she

68

protested. 'I'll make a sandwich as soon as I've finished talking to you.' Now the subject had been raised, she realised she was feeling peckish, and Nina was right about making sure she stayed healthy. 'Actually, I'm planning a trip to the village store later,' she said, 'so you can stop fretting.'

'That's what I want to hear.' Nina sounded appeased. 'I'm glad your sleep's improving. The island air must be doing you good. Besides, not that I'm being mercenary or anything,' she teased, 'but you'll need all your strength for the work you're going to do for us.'

'There's that ruthless streak coming out again,' Rosa laughed. 'I should have known.'

While Nina chatted on, she wondered if she would ever stop mothering her. She smiled to herself; probably not. It went without saying that Nina had her best interests at heart, as Rosa did hers. With her parents away in Spain at the time she'd discovered Nick's betrayal, Nina had been the first person she'd gone to for support.

The memory of Nina's reaction — disbelief, concern, and then pure outrage — was still clear in Rosa's mind. She'd had a real battle on her hands to stop Nina going round to the office right then and telling them both what she thought, but finally Rosa had got the message across that it would be far more productive if Nina went with her to the flat she and Nick shared, and helped remove her belongings.

Rosa recalled her words. 'You'll be staying with us while you decide what you're going to do,' she'd said. 'You're not staying at your parents' house on your own while you're dealing with this.'

She had known Nina was right. At the time she had needed her best friend's help. She wondered whether to tell her about Nick's call and the way he'd tricked her into answering, then decided to leave it for the time being.

'So, have you seen anything of Gareth after last night's escapade?'

Rosa groaned. 'I wish I'd never

mentioned it. I'm never going to live that down, am I?'

'Nope.' Nina chuckled. 'Well, not for a while yet.'

'Actually, he took me to Llangefni this morning to get the paint I needed.'

'Did he now?'

Rosa immediately sensed Nina's radar switch on and gave a silent groan. 'He had some business in town so he offered me a lift, that's all. He seems well over finding a strange woman asleep on his sofa.'

'I'll bet he was just being polite.'

'Probably,' Rosa agreed. 'Anyway, let's change the subject. Thanks to him I got you a good discount.'

'Did you!' Nina exclaimed. 'That's great. You will thank him for me, won't you? So what did it come to? I'll write a cheque out now and post it to you. I don't want you out of pocket on our behalf.'

'You don't have to bother about it just now,' Rosa insisted. 'My bank balance is fairly healthy, and will be better still when the company finances have been sorted. I'm just waiting to hear from Emma about signing the final papers. Remember, she said it could be any day now.'

'I remember,' Nina said. 'The sooner the better as far as I'm concerned. I can't help worrying Nick will do the dirty on you and somehow fiddle things to his advantage.'

Rosa frowned; she had feared the same. 'I'll be surprised if he gets the better of Emma,' she said. 'She's a brilliant solicitor, made my head spin with her knowledge of company law. She raised points I'd never even thought of. You and Paul did me a huge favour putting me on to her.'

'That's what we're here for,' Nina said softly.

Rosa swallowed against a sudden ache in her throat. She was sure that if Nina had heard anything about Kirsty and Nick's rocky relationship, she would have mentioned it. She shook their image from her mind. 'Anyway, enough about me; what have Chloe and Eva been up to lately?'

'I'll bring you up to date once you've promised me you'll drop the idea of doing any more work today, and put your feet up after you've done your shopping.'

She's right, Rosa thought, glancing out of the window. Despite the gorgeous day outside, it wouldn't be long before the natural light started to fade. It made better sense if she made an early start in the morning.

'Promise,' she repeated.

'Good. Right; you won't believe it, but Eva got a star today for being the best-behaved in class — which didn't please Chloe that much . . . '

Rosa laughed as she listened to the story. Talking to Nina was better than a tonic.

3

Hands on hips in the centre of the bedroom, Rosa stretched her aching back and studied the ceiling. With white paint covering the original faded pastel pink, and the walls glowing with a warm honey tone, it looked so much fresher.

More than satisfied with the results of the morning's work, she realised she was practically grinning with pleasure; something she knew she'd not done in a while.

In her mind's eye, she had a complete picture of how the room would look when finished, with its seaside theme of white woodwork, a warm varnish on the floorboards, pretty rugs and curtains, and maybe some traditional bedroom furniture painted powder-blue. She was sure the girls would like it.

She reminded herself to ask Gareth if there were any auction salerooms on the island. She had been aware of him coming and going from the farm a number of times yesterday, and also that morning; sometimes with Ifan, sometimes alone. He'd appeared so preoccupied she'd baulked at distracting him then.

Despite trying not to, she couldn't help but continue to wonder about him and Erin. On first impressions she came across as not being his type at all. In Rosa's opinion, haute couture didn't gel with life on a farm; but then, she asked herself, what did she know about farming?

A sudden loud knocking on the front door startled her. Was it Gareth? Who else could it be? For one heart-stopping moment, she contemplated that it might be Nick, then told herself to stop being ridiculous. But was she just being paranoid? After all, from what he'd said the other day, he'd been searching her out.

He knew of Paul and Nina's cottage

on Anglesey; the sale had finally gone through the month before she and Nick had split up. But did he remember where it was situated?

No, she decided, he would have forgotten all that by now . . . wouldn't he? Pushing her fears aside, she hurried downstairs.

Her worries disappeared completely when she saw Gareth standing there. Her sudden breathlessness, she told herself, was due to having raced down the stairs.

She met his eyes briefly, not wanting to linger in their dark depths.

'I was just wondering how you were getting on with the decorating, and if the offer of a coffee still stands,' he said.

'Of course it does,' she smiled. 'I was just thinking about putting the kettle on, so you couldn't have timed it better.' She opened the door wider to give him room. 'Come on in.'

'I'll just leave these by the step.' He bent over and began to pull off his wellingtons.

'You don't have to . . . ' she began, then saw the soles were thick with mud. 'Then again,' she grimaced, 'maybe you should.'

He smiled up at her. It was infectious. Then he stepped into the hall. The familiar smell of fresh air was about him, mingled with a faint astringent scent of soap. She also noticed a hole in the toe of one of his thick tweed socks. Overriding all of it was her awareness of the confines of the narrow hallway once he was inside.

She inched back. 'Looks like dirty work.'

He gave her a wry look. 'I've been checking some of the boundary walls. Bad weather can undermine them,' he explained, 'and the fields are still a bit of a quagmire in places. You wouldn't thank me for bringing half of them inside.'

'No, I guess I wouldn't,' she agreed lightly. 'Anyway, I'm glad you knocked. I've wanted to see you.'

Was that a flash of pleasure she

sensed in the slight widening of his eyes?

'Why's that?' he asked.

'There are a few things I want to search out, so I need to pick your brains again — if you don't mind, that is.'

'Why should I mind?' He hoped his disappointment wasn't showing. He'd expected something else — but what, he really couldn't say. 'I'll either be able to help you or not.'

He cursed silently; he hadn't meant to sound so pedantic. When she opened the door she had appeared pleased to see him, but now her expression told him a barrier had just gone up.

'True enough,' she said, a little stiffly. 'I was wondering if there were any auction rooms on the island. I was thinking of picking up a few bits and pieces for the cottage ... something with character.'

'Hard one first,' he joked, in an attempt to lighten the atmosphere. He got the feeling it hadn't worked. He cleared his throat. 'The main auctions are held just outside Llangefni. The local paper prints a notice of the dates and what's coming up for sale.'

She brightened immediately. 'That's great. I'll pick up a copy.'

'It looks like you've made a start on the work.'

She realised he was looking at her outfit. 'Oh, you mean these?' She glanced down at the white bib-and-brace overalls which loosely covered her jeans and navy T-shirt. They were marked here and there with colourful paint splashes. 'I'm not really a messy worker,' she said. 'I've just had these for a very long time.'

He smiled and cocked an eyebrow. 'Sure,' he teased.

She met his challenge with a grin. 'Come upstairs and I'll prove it.'

Her challenge had him immediately thinking along completely different lines! *Easy*, he warned himself, as she headed for the staircase.

'Well, if you think Nina and Paul won't mind. It's their cottage now.'

She turned her head, sending her

thick ponytail swinging. 'Of course they won't mind,' she dismissed lightly. 'You can tell me if I missed any bits in my paintwork. I've almost finished the girls' room,' she added, as she led the way up. A few steps along the landing, she disappeared through the open doorway into one of the front bedrooms. As he followed after, she halted in the centre of the empty room and turned to face him. 'What do you think?'

The anticipation in her tone touched him. She waited while he studied her efforts. Eventually he said, 'I don't recognise the place.'

Is that a compliment or not? she wondered.

Then she got her answer when he added, 'It's amazing. It looks so much bigger now, and the colour on the walls makes me think of the beach.'

'Yes!' she exclaimed happily. She glanced out of the window. 'That's exactly what I was trying to achieve: an echo of the distant sands as they curve towards the headland.'

'Very poetically put,' he said.

She couldn't help but laugh.

'No, seriously, I'm impressed.' He smiled down at her. It was good to see that the dark circles beneath her eyes were fading, and she seemed in a happier mood today. It warmed his heart to see a glow in her expression.

After hearing part of her phone call the other day, he had gained some insight as to why she appeared so troubled. What sort of idiot had she been engaged to? Maybe, before she left, he'd find out.

Why did the thought of her leaving bother him so much? He switched off that negative line of thought.

'I might even steal a few of your ideas when the barn conversion gets underway,' he joked.

When . . . not *if*? That's it, he told himself, be positive. Although finances would be stretched, he'd work round it somehow.

Rosa's interest was immediately taken. 'D'you mean the old stone barn?'

He nodded. 'Yes, that's the one.'

Her eyes lit up. 'I thought *conversion* the first time I saw it. Will the work be starting soon?

His expression changed. 'The plans are going before the council at the end of next week. From what I've been told, there shouldn't be a problem, but I still have to get things sorted . . . in my head, I mean: try to work out the costings in the most economical way without cutting corners, work out a schedule, that kind of thing. That's the main headache. I'm depending on it being up and running before the main holiday season is over, to generate some extra income — and, of course, there's the farm to run as well . . . ' He shrugged despondently. 'Sometimes I think I've bitten off more than I can chew.' Reading genuine interest in her expression, he felt a sudden need to confide. 'The bank didn't come up with all I'd hoped for, you see, so some rejigging with the financing will have to be done.'

That was what he was doing in Llangefni, she guessed. An idea began to form. Her work was going so smoothly, she knew she would have it done with weeks to spare. Should she go for it and make the suggestion? Why not? She had nothing to lose. She took a breath . . .

'I could help out if you're stuck.'

He looked slightly puzzled.

'But surely you do your decorating thing when everything else has been done?'

'It's not all I do,' she said. 'I come from a long line of builders; my father and his two younger brothers run the family business now, although Dad's semi-retired. I was torn whether to join the company or concentrate on interior design. In the end, design won out and I studied that at uni, but I carried on helping in the office during the holidays and learned the business inside out. Then I met Nick and we formed our own company. I've worked on new builds, conversions, large ones, small ones, practically the lot.'

Gareth noticed the change in Rosa's tone when she mentioned her ex's name. She was obviously still hurting. Aside from that, though, he couldn't believe what he was hearing about her knowledge of the building trade. It was too good to be true.

Rosa could see she'd caught his interest. 'We could talk some more while I make the coffee.'

'Sounds good to me.'

As he followed her downstairs, he still had trouble trying to process what she'd told him. Was it possible Rosa was the answer to his problems? *Slow down,* he warned himself.

'Milk and sugar?' she asked as she opened a cupboard and took out the jar of coffee.

'Black, with two sugars, please,' he said. 'Helps keep me awake if there's a problem with the lambing. Sometimes it's an effort to get up in the early hours to check them out in case there's a complication.'

'Does that happen often . . . problems, I mean?'

'Can do,' he said. 'Sometimes a lamb can be sickly, and despite every effort we lose them. After a difficult birth, it can be the ewe that doesn't recover and the lamb survives. If we can't find a potential adoptive mother pretty quickly, we have to bottle-feed. Still, the new stock I bought last year is a tough breed, and they don't need as much shepherding as the ones Dad always had. Eventually they will be well worth it.'

'But waiting for it to happen adds to the pressure,' she said, echoing his thoughts.

With her understanding, his worries shrank a little. 'I'll get there in the end.' He shrugged. 'There's no doubt about that — I just hope the end's sooner than later.'

'I'm sure it will be,' she encouraged.

While Rosa waited for the kettle to boil, she began to tidy away the plans and sketches for the cottage she'd left scattered over the kitchen table, and she realised Gareth was looking at them with interest.

'My ideas for Ty Newydd,' she explained. She offered them to him. 'Take a look while I make the coffee, if you like. Pull out a chair and make yourself comfortable.'

'Thanks,' he said. 'Mind if I take off my jacket? It's a lot warmer in here than outside.'

'Go ahead,' she invited. 'Sorry I haven't any biscuits. I'll stock up later when I shop.'

He unzipped his jacket and hung it on the back of his chair, then sat down and picked up her drawings. There was a comfortable silence while he studied each sheet in turn. When she carried the two steaming mugs over to the table, it gave her a good feeling to see he was so absorbed with her sketches he'd not noticed she'd joined him. She placed his drink carefully to one side then slipped silently onto the chair facing him.

Contentedly nursing her mug with

both hands, her eyes traced his features, the strong line of his jaw and the thick black lashes any woman would die for, which now shaded his eyes as he studied her work. Even if she'd not known his profession, she'd have guessed his healthy complexion and muscular body indicated an outdoor life.

After just four days, she knew she had only scratched the surface of Gareth Pritchard; but, despite a few prickly moments, she had to admit she liked what she saw. *'Like' being the operative word*, a small voice warned; she could never allow herself to think of him in any other way. Once bitten, and all that . . .

As he placed another sheet onto the growing pile in front of him, he was suddenly aware she had joined him. 'Sorry, I didn't realise,' he began. 'These are a real eye-opener.'

His expression showed he was seeing her in a different light, and despite what she'd just told herself, his smile made her heart quicken as she watched him reach for his coffee and take a sip.

Suddenly it mattered what he thought of her work. 'You like them?' she asked.

'I'll say. Makes me realise how unprepared I am for this project, especially the finishing touches. The cottage will be transformed by the time you're done here.'

He took another gulp of his drink. Should he go for it and offer her the work? His mind began to race. Was she really capable of overseeing the entire conversion? If she was, her input would take a huge weight off his shoulders, since it was looking more and more like one hell of a job to get right — but get it right, he must.

'Were you really serious just now about the conversion?' he asked.

Rosa was suddenly aware that the lightness had gone from his tone, and her stomach gave a tiny flip; the importance of this new source of income was so clearly written in his expression that she had an uncharacteristic attack of nerves. She swiftly reminded herself of what she had already achieved with her own business.

'Yes, of course,' she said. 'I understand costings, work schedules, site management, and so on. I know the sequence of a build inside out, and I love seeing what starts out as an idea on paper become a reality. We had contracts for numerous conversions last year. There was an understanding it was his domain, but I always had an input, even more so when I was contracted to do the interior styling.'

She frowned, her mood suddenly taking a nosedive. Would she ever be free of Nick and go on to make a success of a lone career? She took another sip of coffee. Of course she would. Nina and Paul had often said she'd carried the business. She'd had plenty of time since to look back and realise this was true.

'Won't you be needed back in Norfolk after you've finished here?'

His question broke her train of thought and she frowned.

'I said the other day when you took

me to Llangefni that after we broke up, carrying on the business together was out of the question.'

'That's right, you did, but where does that leave you?'

It was out before he knew it. Immediately he felt a heel when her expression stilled. 'No, sorry,' he hastened to add, raising the flat of his hand. 'I shouldn't have asked; it's none of my business.'

Rosa understood his concerns. If he was considering employing her, it wasn't unreasonable for him to want to know more about her, or any work commitments she might already have.

'It's fine,' she said. 'I understand why you asked. Two weeks before our wedding I discovered he'd been having an affair with our PA. In fact, he'd got her pregnant. Apparently it had been going on for quite some time.'

She looked away for a moment. How could she have never even suspected? It was that more than anything that unnerved her.

Seeing her tense expression, Gareth wished he'd never asked.

'I'm sorry,' he repeated. 'I didn't mean — '

She cut him off with a gesture. 'It's history. You learn to deal with a situation or go under. I'm working independently now. I have some commitments in early summer, but before then, things are pretty much in the air. That's why I'm here for Nina and Paul. There's always work for me with Dad, but I don't need to commit yet. So I have the luxury of some free time after I've finished here.'

Rosa felt so much better for having told him, and went on, 'Anyway, that's how it is, but don't feel pressurised in any way. You should consider at least two other people for the position. With your contacts, there must be someone you know.'

I don't want anyone else. The truth hit Gareth hard as he studied her strained face, but he still felt a heel for raising the subject of her split.

'Rosa,' he said softly, 'I didn't mean to stir up bad memories.'

The concern in his tone made her feel vulnerable again, but she managed to overcome it and even raise the hint of a smile.

'It's OK. I know you didn't.' Those first days when she barely had the energy to pull herself out of bed seemed a lifetime ago; now she could look back at what she'd experienced through different eyes. 'I've come a long way since then, and staying here is a bonus. Anglesey's definitely lifting my spirits.'

'I'm glad you like my part of the world.' *More than glad*, he added silently. After what she'd told him, he knew he'd have to tread carefully. 'Would you like to take a look at the plans and get more of an idea of what's involved? I could show them to you later if you like.'

Rosa's heart skipped a beat — did that mean he was offering her the work? *Don't jump to conclusions*, she told herself.

'I'd love to see them. Why don't you come round for dinner and we could discuss them then . . . if you've nothing planned, of course,' she hastened to add. For all she knew, he might be seeing Erin. The thought was sobering.

Maybe she shouldn't have suggested that. Perhaps it was only business to him.

His face broke into a wide smile. 'What time would you like me to come round?'

'Seven o'clock suit you?'

'Seven o'clock it is, then.' He tossed back the last of his coffee and got to his feet.

While elated by Rosa's invitation, as he returned to the farmhouse, Gareth reminded himself of what she'd been through. Despite what she'd said, it was clear she was still hurting, and probably the last thing she needed right now was a man in her life. He had less than six weeks to change her mind.

* * *

'It's Rosa, isn't it?'

Rosa glanced up, distracted from contemplating whether to choose steak or chicken for dinner, to see Betsan heading her way, pushing a supermarket trolley.

'Hello. It's good to see you.' And she was pleased they'd bumped into each other — Betsan should be able to give her some idea of Gareth's preferences in food.

'I expect you're settled in by now? We might see you at the weekend. The boys want to see their lambs. Gareth let them choose one each the other night; that's why we were there.'

'He was telling me earlier about the barn conversion,' Rosa said, grabbing the opportunity to keep the conversation about him going. 'He's promised to show me the plans later.'

'Oh, I'm glad. He could do with some company other than family.'

'Actually, he's coming round for dinner.'

Betsan's eyes lit up. 'That will make a

nice change for him.'

For me, too, Rosa reflected. 'Is there anything in particular he likes to eat? Or doesn't like?'

'He'll eat whatever you put before him,' she assured her. 'He has the appetite of a horse.'

'Well, that gives me plenty of scope. I'll just make sure there's lots of it.'

Betsan's expression became more thoughtful. 'I'm really pleased you two are getting along. To be honest, I was bothered by his attitude when we found you in the farmhouse. That wasn't like him at all.'

'Don't worry about it. We've both apologised and it's all forgotten now.'

'Good. I just hope everything goes to plan for him with the barn. It's a big job to take on.' She moved a little closer. 'And,' she lowered her voice, 'Erin's pestering doesn't help.'

Rosa's interest was piqued.

'They were going out for a short while; nothing serious — well, not as far as he was concerned, but she just won't let it go. Anyway, enough of her, I'd best get on. It'll be time to pick up the boys from school soon. See you at the weekend, maybe?'

Rosa nodded. 'More than likely; I'll probably be working. So much for wanting to see more of the island; it looks like six weeks is nowhere near enough for what I had in mind.'

'Then you'll just have to take up permanent residence.' Betsan's eyes twinkled.

The comment had struck a chord in Rosa; but after Betsan had gone, she sternly reminded herself that she had been here less than a week, and to consider staying permanently at this stage was ridiculous. If nothing came of her suggestion of working on the barn, come Easter she would be gone and Gareth would be just a memory. What she had to focus on was planning her future back home.

Yet somehow that now felt like a backward step, even though all her family and friends were there.

Driving back to the cottage, she recalled what Betsan had said about Erin and Gareth, and wondered if his sister really had the full picture. From what she'd seen the other day, he had appeared completely relaxed in her company.

Suddenly, Rosa felt totally flat.

* * *

Rosa was taking a chicken casserole out of the oven when she heard a knock on the kitchen door. 'Come in,' she called, placing the casserole on the back of the hob.

She turned to see Gareth step inside, and something stirred in her heart. His hair looked slightly damp and he had a well-scrubbed look about him. His pale cream shirt, of finer cotton than his work shirts, accentuated his dark colouring, and charcoal jeans covered his long muscular legs. She also noticed a large manila envelope tucked beneath one arm — and he had brought a bottle of wine.

'Something smells good,' he greeted her enthusiastically.

'Thank you. We're having chicken in a white wine sauce, with baby potatoes, sugar snap peas and carrots. And, if you've room for it, apple pie and cream and the cheeseboard to finish.'

His eyes widened and he grinned.

'Lead me to it.' He immediately set to opening the wine and pouring a glass for them both.

'Best leave mine there,' Rosa said over her shoulder. 'I have my hands pretty full at the moment, but don't let me stop you.'

Gareth picked up his glass and leaned against the worktop, watching while she drained the pan of potatoes then shook it over the burner for a few moments to dry them off.

Despite telling himself earlier that tonight would be business only, the minute he saw her, his intentions had crumbled. Tendrils of her beautiful copper hair framed her face, while the rest was loosely held back with a tortoiseshell grip. Every shade of green appeared to be in the slim-fitting multi-patterned top she was wearing over black trousers. He had never seen a woman look so beautiful. As he took another drink from his glass, she broke into his thoughts.

'Thank goodness Nina's organised,' she said.

He frowned, wondering what she meant.

'You look perfectly in control to me,' he said, as she added a knob of butter and a few pinches of dried mixed herbs to the potatoes, then gave the pan another good shake.

'No, what I meant was . . . ' She threw him a smile. This time, the effect on him was more powerful than the wine. ' . . . I'd not thought about wine glasses when I was in the supermarket. Luckily there were a few in the cupboard along with the crockery.'

Gareth came back down to earth. 'Oh, I see. Well, if you find yourself short of anything, come round and check out what I have before you go shopping. There are all kinds of things that never get used now from one year to the next.'

'Thanks, I'll do that,' she said as she began to serve up. She was touched by what she'd just heard. His life must have been very different when the family were all together in the farm-house.

He took the chair across from her, raised his glass and said, 'To future plans.'

'To future plans,' she repeated as their glasses clinked together. She glanced at the envelope he'd placed on the far end of the table. 'And I'm really looking forward to studying your plans, too,' she quipped, 'but not until after we've eaten.'

'Good,' he exclaimed. 'I'm starving.' He picked up his knife and fork and began to tuck in eagerly. After a few moments he looked at her and said, 'This is the best meal I've tasted in a long time.'

'Thanks again.' She smiled. 'It's not a

complicated dish. I'll show you how to make it, if you like.' She was met by an overplayed horrified expression. 'So you're not a new-age man, then,' she challenged light-heartedly.

'I can do beans on toast, cheese on toast, eggs on toast . . . '

Rosa laughed spontaneously and realised she hadn't felt this relaxed in a very long time indeed.

* * *

When the meal was over, Gareth unfolded the blueprints and smoothed them out on the table.

'So this is what the architect came up with after we'd tossed a few ideas around,' he said.

Eager to see what he had in mind, Rosa scanned the drawings, admiring the quality of the draughtsmanship and the design. 'Excellent,' she murmured as she absorbed the details.

'You think so?' He sounded both pleased and relieved.

'Yes,' she said, looking back up at him, flattered her opinion mattered. 'Oh, before I forget, I've drawn up a list sequencing the main stages of a build for you; but as I've not seen inside the barn yet, there may be a few alterations. The contractor will know all this, of course, but it'll give you a fair idea of what's involved before things get started.'

She went over to the dresser and opened a folder she'd left there. 'This is it.' She gave him a sheet of headed paper. 'Ignore the business details; apart from my mobile number they no longer apply.' She realised she'd said this without any sense of regret.

He glanced at the stylish heading, giving the company name, address, and several phone numbers, before reading what she'd written. 'Great,' he said. 'I'll keep it safe with the plans. I have a few ideas in mind for one or two of the outbuildings, too,' he continued, 'provided all goes well with the barn, that is.'

'I'm sure everything will be fine,' she

encouraged. She glanced back at the blueprints. 'Whoever drew these up for you knows their business. You've not made the common mistake of trying to squash too much into the available space. I came across this time and time again when speculators bought up properties to convert into flats.'

Nick, she'd come to discover, had begun to think along those lines, too, and tried on more than one occasion to convince her how lucrative it would be for them, but she would have none of it — even though it had caused them to row. Maybe, she reflected, that was when the first cracks formed in their relationship. She shook the memories away and glanced at Gareth again. 'It's good to see something well thought through.'

Gareth nodded, encouraged by her agreement, yet his expression was deeply serious.

'It's got to work. The survival of the farm depends on it.'

4

Rosa's concentration on applying a coat of white gloss to the top of the rear bedroom window frame was broken when, above a background of farmyard noises, she heard Gareth call her name.

She glanced down through the glass to see him standing in the yard, waving a letter at her and looking particularly pleased with himself.

'It's official,' he called. 'The plans passed.'

'That's brilliant,' she shouted down happily. 'Come in. I'll be down in a minute.'

She quickly finished the section she was working on, then tore off a piece of film wrap from the roll she kept among her tools and wrapped it round the paintbrush to prevent it drying out.

After what she'd said to him about managing the conversion, she had been working long hours to make more headway with the decorating just in case he offered her the job of site manager.

Gareth had had his hands full with the ewes, and she wondered how many days it had been since they'd last had anything like a real conversation; it had been close to a week since she'd cooked for him. With anticipation growing about his news she raced downstairs where he was waiting for her in the kitchen.

'Take a look,' he said eagerly, handing her the letter. His keenness was infectious and she quickly scanned it. It was brief and to the point, quoting the bare details and confirming approval.

'I'm so pleased for you,' she said, eyes shining. 'I was sure they'd be passed but it's always a relief to have it in writing. Now you can get on with organising everything.'

'The job's yours if you want it,' Gareth said.

As his offer hit home, Rosa experienced an initial flutter of excitement which then turned into an unexpected feeling of apprehension. Suddenly it all seemed a huge responsibility. Through the open window she became aware of the sounds of bleating sheep and the distant cries of gulls calling to each other. Together with his new flocks, the conversion was paramount to the farm's survival. Gareth had said so the night they'd had dinner. If she agreed to do it and something went wrong . . .

'Rosa?'

She blinked and focused on Gareth again. 'I know we didn't nail anything down,' he began, 'but you seemed really keen when I first mentioned it.' He searched her face, his expression strained. 'Why do I get the feeling you've changed your mind?'

Guilt washed over her in waves and she cursed Nick for undermining her confidence. 'No, no, I haven't — but . . . '

'But what?' he prompted.

'You need to get the work started as soon as possible, but I need to finish here.' She was fudging, and she knew it — and he knew it, too.

'That's not a problem. I've yet to confirm dates with the contractor, and from the number of empty paint cans I've seen stacked by the bins, it looks like you're racing ahead.'

For all her self-doubt, she knew she could organise the conversion with her eyes closed, so why the cold feet? The answer hit her hard. Disappointing Gareth in any way was something she would never be able to live with.

She forced herself to meet his gaze. 'I'll have to go back home when Nina and Paul come over for Easter. I can't encroach on their holiday by staying in the spare room, and that would mean two wasted weeks. With your deadline, every day counts.' She handed the letter back to him.

Gareth stuffed it into his back pocket.

'You can always stay in the farm-house.'

'Stay with you?' she exclaimed. 'I couldn't.'

He raised a brow. 'Why not? There

are three spare bedrooms. We'd hardly get under each other's feet.' His eyes narrowed slightly. 'OK. I get it. You're missing Norfolk and have had a change of heart.'

It struck her that she wasn't missing home at all. There was something about the island that gave her a sense of belonging, something about the farm . . . this man. She told herself she was crazy.

'No, it's not that at all.'

'Then what is it?'

Under his steady gaze, she just couldn't find the right words.

'I'd best get started on trying to find someone else, then.' He made to walk away.

'Gareth, wait!'

She reached out and grasped his arm; felt the tenseness of his muscles beneath his sweater. She couldn't let him down. She just couldn't.

'I just want you to be absolutely sure about giving me the work,' she said, 'that's all.'

'I'm more than sure.'

As their eyes locked and the world faded, she felt herself falling readily into his deep, dark gaze. She let go of his arm and lowered her eyes, but then found she was focusing on his lips — and that made things worse. Feelings she thought were long-dead began to stir. She blinked and raised her head again to meet his eyes.

'Then I'd love to be involved,' she said huskily. 'I can't wait to see inside the barn.'

Gareth knew he was grinning like an idiot. He felt like picking her up and swinging her around. But instead he thrust his hands deep inside his trouser pockets and clenched them tightly until he'd calmed down.

'We can do that now, if you like.'

'Can you give me about an hour? I'm in the middle of glossing the back window frames and I don't want to leave them for too long.'

'I'll see you later then,' he said eagerly. His enthusiasm was infectious.

*   *   *

'Hi, Nina — I've a bit of news for you.'

Following a snatched lunch of a cheese salad sandwich, and still excited about her forthcoming involvement in the barn conversion, Rosa had seen she just had time to make a brief call to Nina before she met up with Gareth.

'Good news, I hope,' Nina replied cheerfully. 'How are things?'

'Great. All the bedrooms are done now, apart from the floorboards and — '

'Already?' Nina exclaimed. 'I hope you've not been working all hours for our sakes.'

'No, and even though I say it myself, they look really good. Living-room next, then the hall and staircase, and then I'll be done . . . for now.'

Nina groaned. 'I feel tired just listening to you.'

'I'm having a great time, believe me,' Rosa insisted. 'Have you had any more thoughts about the kitchen and bath-room?'

'Not really. We plan on making a decision when we come for Easter — which reminds me, I've been thinking, it makes sense if you stay over. The three of us can throw ideas around and see what we come up with. There's no point in you travelling back when there's a spare room.

'But I can't be under your feet while you're here on holiday . . . '

'How can you think that? You're part of the family. Chloe and Eva will be so disappointed if you're not there. They're desperate to spend time with you. You're staying at the cottage.'

'Let me finish,' Rosa got in quickly. 'Gareth has just had plans for a barn conversion passed, and I've agreed to act as site manager for him.'

In the silence that followed, she could sense Nina's mind racing.

'That's fantastic news,' her friend said brightly. 'And all the more reason for you to stay. If Gareth doesn't mind, you can show us around and tell us all about it.'

111

Rosa took a breath, anticipating the reaction to what she was about to add. 'I won't have to stay with you, Nina. He's offered me one of his spare rooms while you're all here — and I've said yes.'

This time the silence lasted longer, and she just knew Nina was jumping to all the wrong conclusions. 'It's a working relationship, Nina,' she stressed firmly. 'That's all.'

'Right.' Nina's tone was pensive. 'Yes, of course it is.' She perked up again. 'That's great news. It'll give you a boost to be involved in a project like that. Get you right back into the swing of things before you have to deal with re-establishing your own business here.'

Rosa's mood became more thoughtful. Listening to Nina only reinforced the realisation that she didn't want to rebuild what she'd once had. She wanted a fresh start, and everything was telling her she could get it here. It seemed crazy, but she realised the idea had been buried deep inside from that first morning when she'd opened the bedroom curtains and fallen in love with the landscape.

The reality of actually seeing this through was going to take some serious thinking.

' . . . and the girls are counting the sleeps until the holidays. They can't wait to see the cottage.'

Rosa realised Nina was still talking, and focused again on her voice.

'Would you believe, they've been telling their friends we have our own farm now, and inviting them all to come and stay for sleepovers?' She groaned. 'Life can get so complicated at times.'

Can't it just, she agreed silently. 'Nina, I have to go. Gareth promised to show me inside the barn, and I think that's him knocking now.'

'OK, speak to you soon — don't work too hard.'

* * *

As they approached the barn close up, Rosa could see straight away that it was in excellent structural condition.

'The entrance doors are round the other side.' Gareth indicated them. 'That's where a new track will eventually be opened up for private access, keeping it separate from the farm.' He guided her around the side of the building where, beyond an impenetrable gorse hedge, another stunning view of the coastline opened up before them.

Once more she was impressed. This alone would bring people to holiday here. She stood for a moment enjoying the view, then the sound of the barn doors opening caught her attention. With growing interest she studied the façade. The two arched entrances on the front elevation, she recalled from the plans, were clear; one had been bricked up, leaving the other to form the main doorway. They were perfect for the planned patio windows.

'After you.' Gareth gestured her inside.

Her first impression was of a good

earthy smell, lots of space and a cool, dry atmosphere where, high above them, dust motes danced in the rays of sunlight streaming in through a patterned run of air bricks in the facing wall. There was more than enough height for the planned first floor bedrooms.

As her eyes adjusted to the shadowy interior, she had a further impression of a huge sense of space. Several old farm tools still hung on the thick stone walls, while others lay forgotten in corners. At the far end stood an old-fashioned tractor which appeared not to have been used in decades.

'What do you think?' Gareth asked anxiously.

'It's perfect,' she enthused as she walked further inside.

'Watch your step,' Gareth suddenly called out.

Carried along by her eagerness, Rosa hadn't seen a coiled length of rope lying discarded on the hard earth floor. As her foot became entangled the world suddenly shifted, her reaction to save herself sending the plans flying from her grasp.

She heard Gareth's sharp intake of breath and then he was in front of her, his arms around her. The warmth and power of his body sent shockwaves tingling from her head to her toes. Pressed securely against his woollen sweater she felt his heartbeat merge and race with hers.

'Thanks,' she gasped.

She shook her hair from her face and looked up at him, ready to make some kind of joke about not looking where she was going; but as their eyes met, her mouth went dry, and humour was the last thing on her mind.

'Rosa,' he breathed, and as he lowered his head her lips parted. With his body pressed so firmly against her own, she welcomed the sensations every powerful contour brought. Then his kiss deepened, becoming more demanding, and somewhere beyond bliss, she suddenly realised what was happening.

Her eyes snapped open, and with a gasp she pulled away to stare back at him, wide-eyed.

Confusion raced across his face and his heart sank at her stricken expression.

'Sorry . . . ' His breathing erratic, he ran a hand through his hair. *Are you crazy?* he asked himself. *Coming on to a woman who is still getting over a broken engagement?*

Heart racing, Rosa knew she had to take control. She took a breath. 'You don't have to . . . ' She faltered. ' . . . apologise.' She took a deep, shuddering breath. 'It was just a kiss, Gareth. Don't beat yourself up about it,' she said in a voice she didn't quite recognise as being her own.

Only it wasn't just a kiss, was it? She had never been kissed like that before.

A frown scored his brow; his eyes raked her face. 'Oh well, that's all right then,' he growled.

Rosa was shocked by the intensity of her responses to him, and the dizziness didn't help. The last thing she wanted right now was a relationship . . . especially with a man who appeared to be already taken.

Gareth looked away. 'I'll make sure the floor is cleared of everything before you come in again.'

'Thank you,' she said, still shaking inside.

He walked over to where the plans lay, still silently berating himself, a slight trembling in his hand as he picked them up. He couldn't believe he'd taken advantage of the situation in such a way. After warning himself to take things slowly, he'd let his body rule his head. He wished he knew what she was feeling. Nothing like what he was experiencing, he guessed.

He was bewitched, totally and utterly, but instead of being able to let his feelings be known, he had to rein them in and dismiss them — just as lightly as she had — but . . . Was it wishful thinking? Every fibre of his being was telling him that her response had equalled his own.

'Have you seen all you need to for now?'

Rosa had been trying to concentrate on the interior again, but it was hopeless. All she could think of was his kiss.

She turned and shot him a glance. 'Yes. I'll make a start on the work schedule and costings later. First on the list will be a new concrete floor. There's nothing to stop us going ahead with that. Have you decided on a contractor yet?'

'I hope to get Rod Griffith. He did some repair work for me last year on one of the other barns. I know it's early days, but if you agree, we could probably give him the contract for most of the work.' He gave her a half-smile. 'He's a man of few words but many talents, and has a good team. Trouble is, he's always in demand, so getting him soon might by tricky. Still, that's my problem. I'll find out when he can come and take a look. I think you'll get on well with him.'

'Sounds promising,' she said, thankful her heart rate had almost returned to normal. She was still having trouble holding his gaze for longer than a few seconds. 'Let me know when he can make it. I can work around what time suits him.'

They made their way back outside into the sunshine, where she waited while he secured the barn doors again, then together they walked back down to the farmyard in silence.

He was still finding it a struggle to think straight. The truth refused to go away. From the moment he'd held Rosa in his arms, everything had slotted into place. And her kiss! Now he understood the expression 'being blown away'.

He reminded himself of her situation. But he'd be damned if he'd leave it there. He'd suggest dinner that evening; say it was to celebrate launching the project. The possibility of discovering then if he had any sort of chance with her both thrilled and scared him.

'Is there anything else we need to talk

about for the barn?' he asked as she paused by the kitchen door. He was hoping she'd invite him in to go over a few more details. He'd grab the opportunity to ask her then.

She frowned as she shot him a glance. 'I don't think so. We can do all that once you've settled on a builder.'

'Yes of course,' he agreed, his hopes fading. Damn it! He fought his disappointment, and decided to go for it anyway.

'Rosa,' he began, 'I just wondered if — '

'Gareth, there you are!'

Talk about timing. Teetering up the yard on the highest pair of heels, Erin picked her way between a covering of muddy tyre tracks and small pools of rainwater.

Gareth's heart sank. He closed his eyes briefly. *Why now?* he groaned silently.

Before he knew what was happening, she had flung her arms around his neck and planted a heartfelt kiss on his lips.

'Hey, what's all this for?' he said, coming up for air. He reached up and eased her hands away, at the same time throwing Rosa a weak smile across the top of Erin's head.

Rosa wished the ground would swallow her up. Moments ago she had willingly surrendered to his kiss, but now here he was in the arms of another woman, and giving her a look that said he couldn't help them falling at his feet — in her case, almost literally.

Erin pouted as she gazed up at him and fingered her gold necklace. 'What sort of greeting is that?' she complained sulkily. 'Does there have to be a special reason to kiss you?'

She shot Rosa such a vitriolic look, it almost made her laugh out loud. She was certainly giving her a 'hands off' warning. Her embarrassment swiftly turned to anger. It was on the tip of her tongue to tell Erin she had no worries there.

'You took me by surprise, that's all,' Gareth said. 'You know I've a lot on my mind at the moment, what with the

lambing and the barn conversion . . . '
He shrugged, tailing off.

Rosa just wanted to be gone. She was about to turn and reach for the door handle when Gareth said, 'I've just been showing Rosa the old barn. She's going to do some work on it for me while she's here restyling Ty Newydd.' He threw her a look she would have translated from any other man as a cry for help.

Her instinctive politeness made her pause for a moment, but then it quickly faded as she took in the narrowing of Erin's cold eyes as she looked her up and down.

'Restyling?' Erin smirked. 'Sounds very grand. Somehow the overalls don't go with the image of interior design. You'd look more at home on a building site.'

Rosa's back went up immediately.

'Oh, I've worked on lots of those,' she said lightly, avoiding the temptation to reply in kind. 'And believe me, I've never had so much fun. That's why I'm looking forward to becoming involved with the conversion.'

Initially Erin looked utterly bemused, but her expression hardened quickly. 'Well, it takes all sorts, I suppose.' And with that she turned her back on Rosa. Linking arms with Gareth, she pulled him a little to one side, and Rosa was promptly dismissed.

As Rosa turned to go inside the cottage she heard Erin say, 'I'm just off to lunch with the girls, but I had to come and tell you I finally managed to get hold of Daddy. When I told him about your plans for the barn he was really keen to invest. Isn't that wonderful?'

Rosa's grip on the door handle hardened.

'He'll be back from Cardiff around three this afternoon,' Erin continued. 'He said he'll see you then and you can have a little chat about it. Now come on, take me out of this mucky yard and I'll tell you what else he said.'

Rosa shot a glance in Gareth's direction and her heart plummeted. From what she could see, his expression showed interest. Then he glanced across at her, his face sober. 'I'll get back to you about Rod as soon as I can,' he said.

'Whenever you're ready,' she replied casually, but inside she was still fuming.

Thankful to close the door on the scene outside, she leaned against it, her mind racing. It sounded very much as if Erin's father could offer the financial backing Gareth was concerned about. A third party keen to invest would take away the stress of worrying about the shortfall in what the bank was prepared to loan — but at what cost? Wouldn't Gareth and Erin's relationship put a different slant on things?

Could she work on a project where Erin would no doubt feel she had a right to poke her nose in whenever the mood took her? If that was a possibility, she would have to make it clear she would not work under those circumstances — but then she would come across as petty.

She sighed and moved away from the

door. As she made her way upstairs, the memory of what had just happened between them in the barn angered her further still. What had she been thinking? Hadn't she learned her lesson? From now on, it would be strictly business — and even that could depend on the outcome of Gareth's meeting with Erin's father.

In the rear bedroom, and feeling downright miserable, Rosa gently brushed the bottom of the freshly-painted window frame with her index finger. Good, it was touch-dry. There was nothing more she could do in here today.

Lost in thought, she made her way into the sitting room and stood staring out of the window, but the beauty of the landscape had little impact.

Then she saw Erin and Gareth walking over to where she had parked her car. Irritation flared when she saw Erin reach up to kiss him again.

With a sigh, Rosa turned away from the window; but, much to her annoyance, she couldn't stop thinking about the other woman. Erin came across as being used to getting her own way. A grown woman who still called her father 'Daddy' was probably spoilt rotten from the word go. Despite her mood, Rosa smiled; she could just imagine her own dad's reaction if she called him that.

It was none of her business how Gareth financed the work, but something was telling her he should tread carefully when considering this offer. Despite everything, the possibility of him making a wrong decision mattered to her. Purely because she hated to see anyone's dreams go awry, she told herself.

Needing to clear her head and raise her spirits, Rosa decided to go out for a walk. Her gaze fell on the small pile of tourist information leaflets lying on a small side table near to the sofa. She had spotted them in the supermarket the day she and Betsan had bumped into each other, and was sure one gave details of a nearby access point onto the coastal path. Just as she found the leaflet she was looking for, her mobile rang.

She tensed immediately as she picked it up. With the threat still hanging over her that it might be Nick, she checked the number, but the screen told her it was her solicitor.

'Emma?' Rosa forced herself to be cheerful. 'How are you?'

'Oh, busy as ever,' Emma replied pleasantly. 'I'm ringing with some good news. The final figure for your entitlement on the close of business has arrived from the accountants. Despite the continuing objections from your ex-partner, they've confirmed my conclusions that he had no grounds whatsoever and you have your full entitlement. Of course, that's partly due to you putting in the majority funding when the business was created.'

Rosa remembered the time like it was yesterday. She'd had no qualms about using the endowment policy her grandparents had invested for her twenty-fifth birthday. Despite the pain the memories brought, the day of the launch still remained with her. There had been so much excitement; she and Nick were going to take the region by storm and become the most successful property developers of all time. Three years later, like a house of cards, it had all tumbled down around her.

'Oh, and I just want to confirm that you have agreed to settle the outstanding balance on the lease for your offices,' Emma added.

'Yes, that's right,' Rosa agreed, reflecting on how lucky they'd been to have taken over a lease which had only a few years to run before renewal. 'I need to cut all ties with Nick, so I'm more than happy to do so.' From her first consultation she had had no problem in being completely open with Emma about the breakdown of their relationship.

'You're doing the right thing,' Emma said with some sympathy. 'Right, all I need now is for you to call in and sign the paperwork, and you'll be done and dusted. The bank will deal with everything after that. It shouldn't take more than a couple of weeks for everything to be finalised.'

'That's the best news ever,' Rosa enthused as a feeling of relief washed over her — at last she could see an end to it all. 'But there's a slight problem. I'm working on Anglesey at the moment, and could be here for some time. Is there any chance of you posting them to me?'

'Not really. I have to witness your signature.'

'Of course,' she acknowledged. 'Sorry. I'm not thinking straight.'

'As much as I'd like a break from the office, it's just not possible for me to come to you any time soon. I've a pretty heavy caseload at the moment.'

'Oh, I wasn't expecting you to do that.'

'It could be put on hold until you return.'

'No it needs to be done right away.' The last thing Rosa wanted was to deal with Nick's reaction to any delay on her part. For her own state of mind she was desperate to have everything wrapped up swiftly. 'If you could fit me in tomorrow, I'll drive back first thing and call into your office.'

'Tomorrow's out, I'm afraid. But I've a slot on Friday at two o'clock.'

'Thanks, Emma. Friday it is . . . two o'clock. Look forward to seeing you.'

Feeling uplifted, Rosa disconnected the call. On paper, she was almost free of the past, and in time Nick would become a distant memory. She would look on things differently, and most important of all, she would get her life back. She knew she had at last turned a corner — but around that corner she'd met Gareth Prichard.

Her fingers trembled as she touched her lips tenderly and relived his kiss. How could she have responded so eagerly, knowing he was in a relationship with another woman? From now on, apart from work, she would keep her distance. The scene in the yard couldn't have come at a better time — she now knew exactly how things stood.

Rosa was beginning to see Gareth in a different light: his attitude towards women was not a million miles away from Nick's. *No, that wasn't fair*, she argued. Deep down, she knew he could never be that self-centred. In the short time she'd known him, she just knew it wasn't in his nature. Yet she thanked Heaven she'd made no more of a fool of herself than she already had.

* * *

Rosa knocked firmly on the back door of the farmhouse, then checked her watch again. There was plenty of time to tell Gareth she would be away for a few days before he left to keep his appointment with Erin's father.

She had been in two minds about whether to tell him of her trip back home. At first she'd considered just packing a few things and leaving, but in

132

the end her conscience told her she must tell him of her plans before she left.

Despite her resolve to keep things purely on a business level, her intentions crumbled momentarily when the door opened and a smile lit his face when he saw her. He had his mobile to his ear, but he cancelled the call. 'I've been trying to get hold of Rod, but no luck. Come on in.'

She shook her head and remained where she was. 'No, it's alright. I shan't keep you a minute,' she said tonelessly.

His smile disappeared. 'Sounds ominous. Look, if it's anything to do with Erin's attitude, don't take it personally; it's just the way she is with most people — a bit over the top, the way she goes about things.'

Rosa frowned. Was that an apology ... some sort of excuse on Erin's behalf? Well, it didn't wash with her. She dismissed it, giving him a look that said she had better things to think about. 'I just wanted to let you know

I'm going home tomorrow, in case you wondered where I was.'

Gareth looked like he'd been pole-axed.

'You're leaving?' His raw tone surprised her. 'I don't understand . . . '

'Sorry,' she hastened. 'I could have put that better — I don't mean for good.'

His sigh of relief appeared heartfelt; and Rosa knew that, if it wasn't for the fact he had Erin in his life, she would have been flattered.

'Don't scare me like that, Rosa. That's exactly what I thought you meant.'

Despite everything, her heart turned over at the feeling contained in his comment, but she quickly told herself she was being fanciful. He needed her expertise for the build, that was all.

'My solicitor just phoned,' she explained. 'The final paperwork has come through, and she needs to see me.' She shrugged and left it there.

He nodded. 'I see. I'm glad to hear

it's just a visit and you'll soon be able to put it all behind you.'

'I'm only planning an overnight stay, but . . . ' She shrugged. 'Well, you never know, so it could be a little longer.'

His stomach churned again. Surely she wasn't having second thoughts about winding up the partnership with her ex? His blood ran cold at the thought.

'Well, thanks for telling me,' he said. 'I'd have worried not seeing you around and your car not being there. So I'll see you in a couple of days?'

'Yes . . . probably . . . '

That didn't help. 'I'll be glad to see you back,' he said with real feeling.

'Thanks.' Rosa struggled not to feel touched by the sentiment. 'If anything changes I'll call.'

She turned to walk away, but he didn't want her to leave, not yet . . . not ever.

'Rosa,' he called after her. She paused and glanced back. 'There's an old inn in one of the bays not far from here, and the food's great. Would you like to have dinner there tonight?'

She frowned; what game was he playing?

'I wanted to thank you for agreeing to work on the barn,' he added, trying to find a reason she might accept; but from her expression he knew the answer was no, and he shrugged, looking a little awkward. 'It's a bit short notice, but . . . '

'It is a bit,' she agreed. 'I plan to be on the road before seven, so I'd thought an early night . . . '

He forced a smile. 'Of course. I wasn't thinking. Maybe we can go when you get back.'

'Maybe.'

As Rosa walked away Gareth went back inside, a frown firmly planted on his brow.

Something about her manner was different. She hadn't said it in so many words, but after what had happened in the barn, he was sure she was telling him to back off.

Frustrated, he flung himself down on one of the kitchen chairs and put his head in his hands. Why did Erin have to turn up and throw herself at him like that? He really would have to get round to telling her he wasn't interested, but the thought of hurting any woman's feelings — even hers — was something he wasn't sure how to handle. Maybe when Rosa got back from Norfolk he could ask her advice on how to go about it — but then again, he asked himself, would she be interested?

Gareth relived their kiss, and a flare of longing fired his insides. Despite her dismissing it as nothing important, the memory of her response told him otherwise — or was that wishful thinking?

Straightening his back against the chair, he rubbed his brow in an attempt to ease his tension. He had enough on his plate with the farm, the conversion, and Erin's misguided belief about resurrecting something that wasn't even there in the first place. He needed to stay focused rather than have every waking minute filled with thoughts of Rosa. Yet day by day it was becoming easier said than done.

He glanced at the growing stack of paperwork on the table that still needed his attention. Frustration flared again. It could wait. He pushed back the chair; he'd check the ewes and work off his mood by doing something physical instead.

★   ★   ★

Inside the cottage, with her thoughts still full of Gareth, Rosa picked up her phone and rang Nina. Her friend's cheerful response raised her spirits a little.

'I heard from Emma this morning,' she announced. 'She's just had the final figures from the accountants and needs my signature on some paperwork. I'm seeing her Friday, but I've decided to drive back tomorrow and stay over at Mum and Dad's for the night. Don't worry,' she hastened before Nina kicked off, 'I'll call round and see you before I come back here.'

'And not include us in your celebrations?' Nina exclaimed. 'You've got to be kidding. And aren't they still away? What's the point in staying in an empty house when you don't have to? Stay here instead . . . 'til Sunday if you like; make it a long weekend and then take your time driving back to Anglesey. The roads should be quieter then.'

It made sense, Rosa agreed, contemplating Nina's suggestion; but celebrate? She hadn't looked at it that way. Then it hit her. She should be punching the air and cheering instead of feeling so wrung-out. A wave of emotion suddenly overwhelmed her and she had to reach for a chair.

'Sorry, I wasn't thinking straight,' she admitted as she sat down. Why do a round trip in two days when really there was no need — and who better to toast her future with than her closest friends?

'You're right, of course. It's a brilliant

139

idea. I'm making an early start in the morning so I'll probably get to yours around lunchtime, if that suits you.'

'I'll have something ready. We can catch up on what's been happening here before I have to collect the girls from school. I won't tell them you're coming — leave it as a surprise.'

'That will be great.' Rosa could just picture the twins' reactions when they saw her standing outside the school gates with their mother. 'Right, I'm off to pack a few things. See you soon, then.'

No sooner had she disconnected when her phone rang again. Assuming it was Nina having forgotten something, she answered without checking the readout. 'OK,' she chuckled, 'what have you forgotten to tell me?'

'Rosa, it's vital we talk.'

She froze at the sound of Nick's voice.

'I don't think so,' she said coldly.

It was as though she'd not spoken. 'I've just seen my solicitor,' he said.

'This final settlement; you've got to be joking. You surely don't think I'm not going to fight it, do you? I've been running the business since you left. There's little consideration for that in the final figures.'

Rosa's stomach began to churn at the thought of another confrontation. 'They were the accountants' conclusions, not mine. Do what you think best. I just want this over and done with.'

She was just about to hit the off button when his tone changed.

'Sweetheart, think about it.'

'Don't ever call me that again,' she hissed, her anger sparked.

She heard him sigh. 'Can't you see, if we have to go through the courts over this, we'll both end up with virtually nothing and the lawyers will be well in pocket? It just doesn't make sense.'

'There's nothing to stop you from changing the company name and continuing with it. From what I recall, we had projects booked months ahead. Forget it. My mind's made up.'

'I can't do it on my own,' he said quietly. She was stunned. At last they'd got to the truth. 'What I'll be left with will hardly finance them.'

'Then I suggest you find another business partner or an understanding bank manager.'

'You've changed, Rosa.'

'Yes, you're damned right I have,' she snapped back. 'And whose fault is that? Look, I'm seeing Emma Friday afternoon and that will be the end of it, so there's no point in continuing this conversation. Don't call me again.'

'Rosa — '

Amazing even herself, she hung up.

5

Despite a disturbed night, Rosa was showered and dressed by six. When she walked into the kitchen, she knew from the glow behind the curtains that the yard lights were on.

Gareth must have the constitution of an ox, she thought as she made a pot of coffee and prepared her breakfast. A spark of hope that she would see him before she left was determinedly crushed before it had a chance to burst into life.

After she'd scooped the last of her muesli from the bowl, she opened the road map she had to hand, and reminded herself of the route she would take. Having done it once before, she was confident her return trip would be a lot easier than the drive there — and hopefully take less time.

A sudden knock on the back door made her jump. Heart thudding, she held her breath. It could only be him. If she didn't make a sound, perhaps he would go away. He knocked again. She told herself to stop being childish, and went to open it.

'I noticed the light was on,' Gareth said after she invited him in. 'So I thought I'd come and wish you a safe journey.'

His jacket looked dusty and there were remnants of straw in some of the creases in the sleeves. The paleness lack of sleep causes angled his features, and the tiny lines fanning his eyes looked more pronounced. Despite it all, she had to fight a sudden urge to reach up and smooth them away.

She blinked. 'Thanks. You look tired. I guess you've had another busy night.'

He told himself he was imagining concern there. 'It was — another fifteen safely delivered.'

If she'd known he'd spent most of the night on automatic pilot, worrying she'd never return, how would she react? Probably laugh and tell him she had a job to do for him, so why would she not come back?

'There's something special when you hear that first bleat from a newborn lamb,' he said. 'And next year will be a lot easier. It's Dad's old flock that mainly needs some attention; the new breed will more or less take care of themselves. I couldn't tell you how many rows we had over investing in them. He would have none of it, but then after he died I found I couldn't part with his ewes until their breeding life was over. It would've felt like being disloyal to his memory if I'd got rid of them.' He gave her a wry look. 'Not very business-minded, I know, but as this is their last season . . . '

'I understand,' she said. 'Sometimes it's not all about business; family matters more.'

His expression sobered. 'I realise that now,' he said. 'But still, I'd like to think he'd approve of what I'm doing. The new breed has an impressive track record.'

'That sounds very positive. Will it mean fewer nights in the sheds for you?'

'Definitely,' he said.

'Well, that's reason enough.' She raised a small smile. 'Would you like a coffee?'

'No, no.' He gestured with his hands. 'I can see you've had yours. I mustn't hold you up. You said you wanted to make an early start.'

'That's true,' she said. But despite her resolve to keep an emotional distance from him, if truth be told, right then she didn't want to leave while he looked so washed out.

She was rapidly gaining a picture of how much of a struggle he had to keep the farm running productively. It certainly put her career concerns into perspective. The least she could do was make him a hot drink.

'The time it takes to have a coffee hardly matters,' she said. 'Oh — I've just remembered. There's half a loaf in the breadbin, and it'll only go stale while I'm away. How about some toast to go with it?'

A smile lit his face and she struggled not to let it affect her. 'You're an angel, Rosa,' he said. 'I must have done something right to have you come into my life.'

★ ★ ★

Driving down the centre of her home town, Rosa looked around at familiar sights. It was a place she knew intimately and had thought would always be home, but now she was seeing it through different eyes.

The island of Anglesey had had such a positive effect on her spirits; but, she asked herself, would she have felt the same if she had not met Gareth? That was something she'd never know. Yet for all her intentions of keeping love on hold, there was no sense in denying that from the first moment their eyes met she had felt something connect. It was almost as if she had found her soul mate.

Hold it right there! Even Nina, a

born romantic, would find that far-fetched. She needed to get back down to earth; stop creating some whimsical scenario of involvement. What mattered most was her work on the cottage and the barn conversion. They would be a brilliant addition to her portfolio for her new business — and her new life.

With what seemed a cruel reminder of the past, the slow-moving traffic eventually ground to a halt just in line with the historic cobbled side street which housed the premises she and Nick once ran their business from.

Despite all she'd been through, she couldn't help but glance across at it. Rosa somehow expected change, but everything was exactly the same. The only difference in the short run of shops was a 'To Let' sign fastened above the gleaming crimson entrance door which led to their first-floor offices. Sadness and loss swept over her and her grip tightened on the steering wheel. Unwanted yet unstoppable images replayed in her mind like a scene in a soap opera. And despite the struggle not to revisit the past, the sounds of the high street faded to silence as she relived that terrible day . . .

*   *   *

Despite battling a bitter December wind, there was a spring in Rosa's step as she walked past the colourful window display in the boutique beneath their offices. Even though she couldn't wait to tell Nick her good news, she stopped short when she saw a jade-green dress taking centre space. With its simple style and hint of silver thread woven into the soft fabric, she knew it would be perfect for her honeymoon — if she could stop herself from wearing it before.

Thoughts of their New Year wedding sent a tingle of happy excitement fluttering in her stomach. She still couldn't believe how smoothly the arrangements had gone.

Nick wasn't expecting to see her until that evening, but she had finished her work — on a new restaurant shortly opening in the centre of town — a day early. The delighted owner had made out a cheque for her there and then, and given a promise of more work in the old country house he and his wife had recently bought.

Rosa had resisted the temptation of calling Nick on her mobile as soon as she got into her car — she wanted to see his face light up when she told him.

With the intention of calling into the shop before she left for home, she turned away and opened the entrance door to the small foyer and set of stairs which led to their offices. She was halfway up the staircase when the sound of Nick's raised voice made her pause. From just above her eyeline she could see his office door was slightly ajar.

Not again, Rosa sighed. Lately he had been giving most people, her included, short shrift. Nina had told her it was probably pre-wedding nerves, and while she thought this a possibility, it still hurt when he sometimes turned on her for no apparent reason.

'You're absolutely sure?' she heard him demand angrily. 'You haven't made some kind of mistake?'

'Of course I haven't.' Kirsty's shrill tone brought a frown to Rosa's brow. Before she could wonder any more about it, Nick's furious response pulled her up short.

'How could you be so careless?'

'Me, careless? What about you? It wasn't all down to me. You're just as much to blame.'

What he said next, Rosa couldn't make out. She started up the stairs, determined to find out what had happened, but when the argument started up again, she hesitated.

'I am not making it up!' she heard Kirsty exclaim. 'I bought one of those testing kits from the chemist in my lunch break. It's positive.'

'Not the local one, surely?' Even from a distance Nick's rage was palpable. 'You idiot — it will be all round town by tomorrow.'

'In that case you'd better tell Rosa pretty quickly then, hadn't you,' she snapped back.

Rosa tried to make sense of what she was hearing. Eventually through a barrier of mind-numbing denial, the truth broke through.

Nick and Kirsty?

Her head began to spin. She grabbed for the handrail as her legs buckled, and eased herself carefully down onto the stairs. For a few moments she thought she was going to be sick. By gradually controlling her breathing she slowly began to overcome the nausea, only for ice-cold shivers to begin wracking her body. She grasped the wooden spindles for support while she stared blindly at the wall, repeating silently over and over again, *It's not true . . . it can't be true.*

How could he do this to her? Why hadn't she sensed there was something between him and Kirsty? Rosa racked her brains searching for clues — gestures, glances, anything — but there was nothing. She had been too wrapped up in their wedding plans to question him having to 'work late' far more often than he ever had before.

With the row still raging above her, Rosa eventually gathered her strength and pulled herself to her feet. Firmly gripping the banister rail, she reached the landing. Once there she straightened her back, took a deep breath, and pulled off her engagement ring before making her way towards his office and opening the door.

* * *

The jarring sound of a car horn snapped Rosa back to the present. She blinked, momentarily flustered, and saw that the traffic in front of her was on the move again. Eager to put the side street and the shocking memories it contained behind her, she quickly put her car into gear. Spurred on by the thought that tomorrow she would finally receive closure, she drove on.

Nina had the front door open wide

and was waving like a mad thing, sending her blonde curls bobbing beside her pretty, round face when Rosa turned onto the gravel drive. She hurried out to greet her.

'I was in the hall when I heard the car,' she beamed. The two women embraced as though they'd not seen or spoken to each other for months. 'It's so good to see you,' Nina repeated, her blue eyes happily scanning Rosa's features. 'I can't believe how well you're looking; your skin's glowing and your eyes have a sparkle about them I've not seen in ages. It can't just be Anglesey, even though I love the place.

'By the way, how's Gareth? I expect you're seeing quite a bit of him now you'll be working on his barn.' Expectation was clear in her expression but Rosa didn't rise to the bait.

'No, not that much,' she countered. 'The lambing season is at its height and he's working non-stop. He looked absolutely shattered when he called round this morning before I left.'

'He called to see you off, then?' Nina asked, not put off, and noting Rosa's concern for Gareth.

'Yes, he did,' she replied, leaving it there and changing the subject. 'I can't wait to see Emma tomorrow and finalise everything, then I'll have Nick off my back for good.'

'And hooray to that. I get the feeling he's still been trying to contact you.'

Rosa nodded. Nina was so perceptive. 'He tricked me into answering once by using a different phone.' Nina's brows arched in surprised concern. 'Then he rang again just after we'd talked yesterday. Like an idiot, I didn't check the number, thinking it was something you'd forgotten to tell me. I cut him short both times.'

'Good for you.' After a slight hesitation Nina added, a little cautiously, 'I heard recently that he and Kirsty are having problems. I didn't know whether to tell you or not.'

'Oh, that's OK.' Rosa brushed her concern aside. 'As a matter of fact, he mentioned it the first time he got through.'

Nina's eyes widened. 'Don't tell me he thinks you'll take him back?'

'He didn't say it outright, but I got the feeling it was there — but it's never going to happen.'

'Damn right it isn't,' Nina exclaimed. 'I can't believe he'd do that! It's ironic really, Kirsty being such a gold-digger and not realising you were the driving force behind the business. Anyway, that's enough of them. You go and settle in while I make a cup of tea, then we can have some lunch.'

'Thanks, Nina,' Rosa sighed. 'I'm more than ready for a cuppa.'

'Need a hand with your bags?'

She shook her head. 'No, I'm fine. They're not that heavy.' She swung one onto her shoulder and picked up the other.

'Don't take too long,' Nina called as she made her way upstairs. 'I want to hear the latest on the cottage and the barn.'

Her thoughts once more full of Gareth, Rosa headed for the spare bedroom and began to unpack.

★   ★   ★

The following afternoon, despite knowing the town like the back of her hand, Rosa allowed herself plenty of time to find a parking space before her appointment with Emma: Friday was market day, which meant spaces were always at a premium. She was beginning to worry if she would ever find somewhere to park when she remembered a vacant plot of land due for redevelopment, not too far from the centre of town. She decided to take a chance.

At the next set of traffic lights, she changed direction, and a short time later she was pleased to see work had not yet begun on the site and there were several cars already parked on the waste ground. She pulled into the next available space.

A quick check of her watch told her she would not have to break into a run to make it on time but she needed to get going. The day was warm, more like summer than early spring, although the shaded side of the narrow back streets held a surprising chill. She shivered and gripped her soft blue scarf closer to the collar of her jacket, eager to be back in the sunshine.

Since the recent opening of a new shopping centre, a growing number of small businesses once located in the High Street had either moved or closed down. As she walked along the virtually deserted pavement, she felt sympathy for the few that were still trading, some having been there for decades, and wondered how long they would survive.

Suddenly she was grabbed from behind and pushed into the recessed doorway of a disused shop. She almost screamed out loud with fright; with her face inches away from a solid wall, she felt the air leave her lungs. She gasped with shock, but before she had time to cry out she was spun round, and found herself staring at Nick's tense features.

'Nick!' she exclaimed, experiencing a confusion of relief and concern. 'What the hell are you playing at? I thought I was about to be mugged.'

'I'm making sure you get things right,' he hissed, his expression taut with anger.

An increasing sense of uncertainty sent her heart thudding even faster.

'Let me go,' she protested. 'You're hurting me.' She tried unsuccessfully to wriggle free from the vice-like grip he had on her upper arms. 'I've told you there's nothing more to be said.'

'Oh yes, there is,' he snarled. 'If you think you can leave me with a pittance from the business, think again.' She stared back in disbelief as his grey eyes bored into hers with a ferociousness she never thought him capable of. 'Believe me — you'll live to regret it if you go ahead with this.'

His tone was so threatening she began to panic. 'Nick, please ... '
Again she tried to struggle free but his

grip on her arms increased, his thumbs digging in so hard she feared he was about to shake the living daylights out of her.

'Do you understand me?' he growled. 'I'm not going to let you get away with it.'

'You alright there, love?'

Rosa almost slumped forward with relief.

The distraction caused Nick's grip on her to ease and she took the opportunity to yank herself free. All she had to do now was get past him and make her way towards the two work-men who were standing at the entrance, looking on with some concern.

Not wanting the situation to develop any further, she forced a smile and said, 'It's nothing, really; just a misunder-standing.'

Neither of them looked convinced.

'You sure?' the older of the two asked. He threw a hard glance at Nick who, she noticed, returned the look in kind.

Rosa glanced back at her rescuers. Despite the throbbing pain in her arms and her heart still beating a tattoo, she managed to nod positively before she edged past Nick and walked towards them. 'Yes, it's fine . . . honestly,' she insisted. 'I have to go. I'm late for an appointment.'

'Going up the road are you, love?' one of the workmen asked.

She nodded and mentioned the name of the solicitors.

Both men exchanged a knowing look. 'That's handy,' the older one said. 'We're fitting out a new estate agent's right next door. What d'you say we keep you company for the rest of the way?'

Her sense of relief was almost overwhelming. 'Why not,' she agreed.

The younger shop fitter glanced back at Nick. 'Make yourself scarce, mate,' he instructed.

With a face like thunder, Nick pushed his way past onto the pavement. 'Don't think this is the end of it,' he muttered to Rosa. 'I know where you're staying. Do what I say or expect a visit.'

Fear shadowed Rosa's eyes as she watched him hurry across the road and disappear down a side street.

'You should go to the police, you know,' the fitter said, looking at her with some sympathy. 'That's threatening behaviour.'

'I'll be fine, honestly,' she assured him, appreciating his concern. 'It was only bluster. I'm just here for the weekend and there's no way he'll call round to the friend I'm staying with. He knows her husband is a muscular six foot four!'

Both men grinned. 'Well, that's alright then.'

Despite what she'd said, as she fell into step with them, she was still shaking inside. She'd never seen that side of Nick before and it shocked her. Despite what she'd just said herself, his threats frightened her.

In an attempt to combat her fears, she began a conversation about the work the two men were doing. 'You were saying a new estate agency is opening up in town. Things must be looking up.'

* * *

'Come in and take a seat,' Emma greeted Rosa after her receptionist had announced her. 'Would you like a coffee? Sarah has just made a fresh pot.'

Still shaken by Nick's assault, coffee was more than welcome. 'Thanks, Emma,' she said quietly. 'Black for me . . . no sugar.'

Emma's brow puckered as she took in Rosa's demeanour. She had expected a more cheerful response now their business was almost concluded. Moments later she turned back to her desk, a coffee in each hand. 'Is there something wrong?' she asked after placing the cups onto her desk.

Unable to relax, Rosa was perched on the edge of her chair, her expression strained.

'It was my own fault,' she suddenly

blurted out, causing Emma to frown. Her thoughts were all over the place, and she was in a quandary whether or not to tell her about what had just happened; but on the spur of the moment, she decided she had to. Despite the fitter's warning, if Nick was still hanging around waiting for her to come out, she could find herself in the same situation — or maybe even worse.

'Nick rang me a few days ago,' she began. 'As you can imagine it ended in a row. I'd just about had enough of him and let it slip that I was finalising everything with you today.'

Emma's concern grew. 'Don't tell me he was waiting for you?'

Rosa nodded. 'Yes. I'd parked where the new office block is to be built,' she began. 'I had no idea . . . ' She took a deep breath. 'He must have been standing in one of the side streets looking out for me, and then he came up from behind and grabbed me, and . . . ' Despite her determination, she couldn't stop the tears coming.

Emma jumped up from her chair, grabbed a box of tissues, hurried round to where Rosa was sitting and pulled out a handful for her.

'I'm so sorry,' Rosa said, with a teary smile.

'There's nothing for you to be sorry about,' Emma said once Rosa had calmed down. 'Would you like me to phone the police? He can't be allowed to get away with something like that.'

Rosa blew her nose, then shook her head. 'I'd really rather you didn't. It could complicate things, and I want this over and done with today — even more so now. I have been thinking about relocating since I've been working on Anglesey — I've come to love it there — and what happened just now with Nick has made up my mind. I'm determined to make a fresh start, so there's very little chance we'll ever see each other again.'

Emma still looked troubled.

'All the same . . . '

'Honestly, I'll be fine,' Rosa insisted.

She managed a wobbly smile. 'I'm staying with Nina and Paul 'til Sunday. Nick guessed I was there, but no way would he come round and try to take on Paul.'

'True enough,' Emma agreed thoughtfully. 'All the same, once our business is concluded, I'll get Trevor, our office manager, to walk you back to your car and see you safely on your way.'

★ ★ ★

With her feet tucked beneath her, Rosa now sat in the corner of one of Nina's comfortable sofas, while she and Paul sat close together on the facing one: both looking at her with strained expressions.

The last thing she'd wanted was to put her worries on their shoulders but she knew she had to tell them about her encounter with Nick. Next time they saw Emma socially, despite her professionalism, being friends there was a chance she might ask about her — and,

Nina being Nina, she would know there was something more behind Emma's enquiry than just small talk.

'No matter what we say, you won't make a formal charge?' Paul asked.

Rosa shook her head. 'I know you both have my best interests at heart and I really appreciate it, but as I said to Emma, it will only complicate things. I'm desperate to have it over and done with, Paul.'

For once Nina remained silent and Rosa gave her a reassuring smile as she went on. 'I'll be back on the island on Sunday and hundreds of miles away from him.'

'And you're considering moving there permanently?' Nina asked, taking in the enormity of Rosa possibly leaving Norfolk for good. 'I'm not trying to make things worse, but after what you said about him knowing where you are staying, it just struck me . . . could he have meant Ty Newydd, not here?'

Nina's words sent a shiver of fear down Rosa's spine. The thought had crossed her mind, but she'd dismissed it just as quickly. To have Nina thinking along the same lines was chilling.

Nina looked at Paul. 'I wish we hadn't talked so much about the cottage. Can you remember telling him where it is?'

'I'm pretty sure we didn't. We've mentioned the village over the years, but I doubt he'd have remembered the name; he wasn't all that interested, was he? As we well know, Nick's idea of a holiday is somewhere far more exotic.'

He gave Rosa a smile of encouragement. 'I'm sure you've nothing to worry about. We'd only finalised the sale about a month before your break-up. I can't imagine him thinking you could possibly be there — or having the time to drive hundreds of miles to seek you out. Remember, he has a business to revive, and Kirsty breathing down his neck to make sure he does.'

Rosa considered what Paul had just said. It made sense. 'And he didn't actually say Anglesey,' she said. 'For all we know, he could be under the illusion I've moved back to Mum and Dad's, and am keeping a low profile.'

Paul nodded, considering her suggestion. 'That sounds more like it.'

'Anyway,' she exclaimed, 'enough of all this; I'm not going to let him spoil the rest of my time with you. So what are we going to do with the girls tomorrow?'

* * *

After Rosa had kissed Paul and the girls goodbye, Nina gave her a final tight hug and a kiss. 'We'll see you soon, then.'

'Of course; I can't wait,' she smiled.

She slipped into her car, switched on the ignition and lowered her driver's window.

'I'll ring you as soon as I get back,' she called over the sound of the engine. 'It shouldn't take me as long this time. It's a perfect day for driving.'

With a wave of her hand, she drove off.

As the car picked up speed and the miles rolled by, Rosa began to relax. Even after the trauma of Friday, the good time she'd had with Nina and Paul and the twins had eventually pushed Nick's empty threats to the back of her mind.

For that was all they were, she decided — just empty threats.

Yet at the same time, she thanked Heaven that her and Nick's plans to book a weekend at a B&B on Anglesey one weekend, so that Nina and Paul could show them their holiday cottage, had never quite materialised.

6

Rosa had barely settled back in when she heard knocking coming through from the back of the cottage. Knowing it could only be Gareth, she frowned at her heart's instinctive reaction.

Bracing herself, she opened the back door, then fought not to let the effects of his obvious pleasure at seeing her show.

'Hi, come on in,' she invited him casually. 'I've not long got back.'

'I heard your car,' he said. He rubbed his boots thoroughly on the mat before walking into the kitchen. 'I just wondered how your trip went.' *Idiot*, he told himself, remembering the reason why she had made the trip. 'That's if you want to talk about it, of course.'

Why not? She decided on the spur of the moment. 'Everything went well and it was lovely to see Nina and Paul and the girls. There's tea in the pot. Would you like a cup?'

'That would be great,' he grinned, jumping at the chance to stay longer. If Rosa was offering tea, it looked like she was also happy to talk.

'Although one thing was strange,' she admitted when they were both settled at the table. 'Everything felt different.' *As though I don't belong there any more*, she added silently. She blinked and focused on him again. 'Which does seem a little ridiculous, after being away for such a short time.'

Gareth felt his hopes rising . . . was she considering a move? He couldn't bring himself to make a joke of asking if she had Anglesey in mind — it meant too much to him, and right now the possibility of her dismissing the idea as ridiculous was a risk he wasn't prepared to take.

Instead, he said, 'Sometimes a place can grow on you without you even realising it.' He took a sip of his tea, fearing if he looked her in the eye she would read the depths of his feelings for her; he'd felt a light had gone out while she was away.

'I suppose you're right,' she said. 'And now I have the pleasure of unpacking.'

So she's not going to talk any more about the meeting with her solicitor, he realised. He felt a rush of disappointment. *Goes to show how much she's prepared to let you into her life,* he mocked himself. He tossed back the last of his tea. 'I'd best leave you to it, then.' He started to get to his feet, adding, 'It's good to have you back, Rosa.'

'Thanks,' she smiled. Despite his relationship with Erin, the sincerity in his tone touched something deep inside. She pushed back her chair and stood facing him. 'It's good to be back.'

He paused for a moment. 'Em . . . I was wondering if you'd be up for dinner tonight.'

A frown flitted across her brow. What was his game? For her own sake, she'd have to turn him down.

'Well, if I wasn't feeling so shattered — but the effort of having to change into something dressier is just . . . ' She tailed off. The disappointment in his expression sent her resolve crumbling.

'You look perfect just as you are,' he said. 'How about we eat at home, and you won't feel you have to get dressed up?'

She'd still have to change out of her jeans and sweater, shower, wash her hair . . .

Gareth sensed her reluctance, but ploughed on. 'Come on. It would save you the bother of having to cook something for yourself.'

Which was true, she reflected.

'I'm not totally useless in the kitchen,' Gareth continued to sell the idea. 'And I've something special in mind.'

Despite knowing she was playing with fire, Rosa gave in. 'Will it be on toast?' she joked.

His offence was obviously feigned. 'It will not!'

'Sorry.' She struggled not to grin. 'In that case, what time do you want me?'

All the time, he answered silently, then blinked the truth away just in case it showed. 'Whatever time suits you? Just come round when you're ready, let yourself in, and then stand back to be amazed.'

'Is forty minutes long enough for you to cook whatever it is you have in mind?'

'Forty minutes is just about perfect,' he beamed.

★ ★ ★

Revived by a long, hot shower, Rosa trawled through the extra clothes she'd thought to bring back with her from her family home. In the end she decided to wear a favourite maroon pinafore dress over a lavender top, with black leggings and black patent pumps. *Worn to death, but still OK*, she mused affectionately as she studied her appearance in an old cheval mirror she'd come across while moving furniture around in the rear bedroom. She brushed her hair until it gleamed, then threw a chunky grey cardigan over her shoulders and went downstairs.

She let herself into the rear of the farmhouse and crossed the flagged utility room which opened onto the kitchen. She knocked on the door before opening it, then paused for a moment in the doorway.

Despite there being no signs of life, the room was cosily warm and welcoming. She shrugged off her cardigan and placed it on the arm of the easy chair near the Aga.

Rosa was touched when she saw the table had been set for two with gleaming cutlery and sparkling glasses; in the centre, an earthenware jug was packed tight with daffodils.

Gareth was right, she smiled to herself. She *was* amazed. And now, after all his efforts, he was probably upstairs getting ready.

With not a bubbling pan to be seen

or any aroma of cooking in the air, she guessed straight away that he'd planned on driving up to the village chip shop. Still, fish and chips were fine by her.

The thought had no sooner entered her head than she heard the front door slamming shut. *Right first time*, she congratulated herself.

He opened the door, looking slightly rushed, and pulled up short. 'Damn. Caught in the act!' he grinned. 'It took longer than I expected.'

Together with his just-scrubbed look, his happy expression made her feel just as happy, too.

'I was hoping to pass this off as my own efforts. And by the way, you look stunning.'

He produced two blue-and-white striped carriers from behind his back and placed them on one of the counters.

'Thank you,' she said. 'Need a hand with the fish and chips?'

'Fish and chips?' he exclaimed. 'Remember, I said it was going to be something special.'

'Of course.' She tried to look serious but failed miserably. 'In that case it has to be a take-away.'

'There's no fooling you,' he said with mock seriousness.

He began to transfer a fair number of foil-topped cardboard cartons from the bag into the oven. Her eyes widened at the amount he'd bought. 'I just need to keep this lot warm for a few minutes,' he said. He strode over to the fridge-freezer and, to her surprise, produced a bottle of champagne. 'We've some celebrating to do first.' He carefully eased the cork from the bottle and began to pour the foaming wine into two champagne flutes she'd failed to notice.

'Celebrating?'

'Celebrating,' he repeated. Looking particularly pleased with himself, he handed her a glass, then clinked his own against it. 'Cheers.'

'Cheers,' she responded.

Behind her smile, a sense of unease began to grow. *He's going to say he's finalised a business agreement with Erin's father*, she guessed, and struggled not to let her disappointment show.

'I managed to get hold of Rod while you were away,' he said, throwing her line of thought into confusion but bringing some relief. 'He's more than keen to do the work. He's been round and taken a look at the plans to see what's involved, and we've discussed a price with some leeway either side, which we're both happy with. His men are going to make a start on digging out the floor tomorrow.' He raised his glass. 'Hence the champagne.'

Rosa relaxed again. 'That's fantastic,' she said. 'I'm so pleased for you.' But concerns about funding still niggled, and her worries were out before she could control her tongue. 'I take it you've come to some agreement with Erin's father about your shortfall, then?'

Immediately, Gareth's expression darkened.

'Sorry,' she said swiftly. 'It's none of my business . . . but after what she was saying the other day, I thought . . . ' She shrugged.

The last thing she expected to see was the warm smile starting to curve the corners of his mouth.

'It is your business, Rosa,' he said. 'And believe me, Henry Martin is the last person I'd go to with any kind of proposition. I'll tell you all about him sometime.' He put down his glass and opened the oven door. 'Now, let's eat; we don't want this to spoil.'

He took out two dinner plates from the oven where he'd left them warming, and placed them on the nearby counter top before taking out the cardboard containers. Since there was room to do so, Rosa began opening them.

'My favourite,' she said as she opened one to find succulent king prawns in a curry sauce.

'That's good,' he grinned. 'I chose a few different dishes, hoping I'd get at least one right.'

Their eyes locked for a moment.

'It's perfect,' she said.

After they had filled their plates, Gareth remembered the champagne and brought the glasses over to the table, handing one to her.

'We're on our way, Rosa,' he said. 'This is going to change everything. I just know it.'

Along with her excitement about the project, one word kept running through her head: We.

It made her feel as if she was going to become part of his life. Despite every ounce of common sense reminding her it was nonsense, that it was all about the build, her desires rebelled, taking her on a road she knew could only lead to heartache.

Brushing the thoughts aside, she raised her glass again. 'To our success,' she said, touching it gently against his and missing a momentary flicker of longing in the depths of his gaze.

'Success,' he repeated.

The champagne went down far too easily, and when he suggested opening a bottle of chilled white wine to go with their meal, she agreed.

As they ate and drank, and Gareth entertained her with farming anecdotes, a soft flush began to warm her cheeks. She listened, fascinated, as he told her more about the cycle of life on the farm. Then, when he mentioned the Martins' land bordered with his, she took the opportunity to satisfy her curiosity.

'You said you were going to tell me about Henry Martin,' she prompted.

He sighed. 'Ah yes, him . . . ' Rosa noticed he didn't look particularly impressed. 'Our families had been neighbours for generations, but when the time came for Henry to inherit, things changed. Dad loved his land and his animals, whereas for Henry it was business, pure and simple — and believe me, he has a head for it. The land next to ours has been rented out to tenant farmers for decades. He's bought up more land in other parts of the island, always renting out, and that's apart from his other business interests.'

It was on the tip of her tongue to ask

about his and Erin's relationship. She held back, but it was as if he'd read her mind.

'Erin thinks her father can do no wrong. She was seven when her mother died, and you wouldn't wish that on anyone.' He sobered a little. 'Henry boarded her out at a school in England, and after that she moved to London to work as a PA. Betsan heard she was living with an investment banker.' He rolled his eyes. 'Which no doubt suited her down to the ground. But then, out of the blue, I bumped into her last December in Llangefni.'

'So, she's left the bright lights and come home for good?' What he said next mattered.

Gareth shrugged offhandedly before tearing off a piece of naan bread and continuing to tuck into his curry. 'I've no idea,' he said a moment later. 'We went out together a few times.' He gave her a wry sidelong look. 'She needed a partner for a Christmas Ball. What can you do when someone goes to the trouble of producing two tickets? She did the same again New Year's Eve.

'Since then she calls in whenever she's around and to be honest I wish she wouldn't,' he added. 'There's no way I'm going to take up her father's offer, so maybe she'll finally get the message.'

He looked so pained, Rosa couldn't help but giggle. 'Maybe,' she echoed, not believing it for a minute. A woman like Erin would not give up so easily. 'Perhaps you should tell her yourself, though. Make it clear you're not interested.'

'I agree,' he said. 'But other things are taking priority right now. I tend to forget about her and then a few weeks later she'll turn up again. I'll get round to it,' he said more to himself than to Rosa, before attacking his curry again.

She left it there, feeling exhilarated that she'd got it wrong and that Erin meant nothing to him. Still, she reflected, he had no idea of the battle he would have on his hands to get Erin to accept the truth.

Eventually Rosa pushed away her plate. 'That was absolutely delicious but I can't eat another thing.'

'Got me beaten, too,' he admitted. 'How about finishing off what's left of the wine in the living room?'

'Why not,' she smiled, getting to her feet.

She settled down at one end of the sofa, he at the other. 'Why not put your feet up,' he suggested. 'You've had a long day.'

She was more than happy to do so. She slipped off her shoes and tucked her legs beneath her. 'This reminds me of my first night here,' she said.

He grimaced. 'And what a welcome I gave you. If you'd taken offence where would we be now?'

'Oh, still getting on with things; me next door, you working all hours through the night. Maybe giving each other the occasional polite greeting if our paths crossed. It would be weird though wouldn't it?' she added.

'Doesn't bear thinking about,' he said quietly.

Expectation crackled in the air but was suddenly gone when she gave an involuntary yawn.

'Sorry, the drive back is getting to me now.'

After taking another sip of wine she realised she didn't want any more.

'Let me take that,' Gareth offered, knowing she was more than ready for bed.

'It was fatal putting my feet up,' she said, shifting position and placing them back on the carpet. 'Now I'm having trouble keeping my eyes open.' She put her shoes back on.

'Come on, I'll walk you back.' He offered a hand to help her up.

'There's no need for you to come with me.'

'Of course there is,' he argued, not letting go of her until they were in the kitchen, where he picked up her cardigan and carefully placed it around her shoulders.

Outside the moonlight silvered the

yard and a chill in the air made her shiver. Gareth slipped his arm around her shoulders. She moved closer to him, relishing the brief contact until all too soon they were at the cottage door.

When she looked up his face was now in shadow. 'Thanks for this evening. I can't remember when I last had such a relaxing time.' She held his arm and stretched up to kiss him on the cheek.

'Neither can I,' he said softly. 'Tonight has been special.'

His quiet intensity touched her. She knew she only had to move closer to him and their relationship would turn into something she was not sure she could handle. The thought was immediately sobering.

'I'd best get to bed,' she said, thankful for the darkness concealing the heat in her cheeks. She eased from beneath his hands just as she sensed he was going to kiss her. 'Night, Gareth,' she smiled. 'I'll see you tomorrow.'

With the closed door between them, Rosa leaned back against it for a moment, her eyes closed, her heart racing. Dare she take another chance on love, allow herself to become vulnerable again?

Unwanted images of Nick and what had happened recently returned — just as a call tone from her mobile alerted her to an incoming text. She frowned. Who could be trying to contact her at this time of night?

Walking over to the table where she'd left it she picked it up but the number was not one she recognised — nor was it the last one Nick had used. Her initial puzzlement turned to concern. The readout showed there had been many texts with barely seconds in between. Could the caller have mistaken her number for someone else's and needed to get in touch urgently?

She steeled herself and touched the screen.

Her eyes widened as she read the stream of vitriolic threats more vindictive than she'd have believed Nick capable of until Friday . . .

Desperate to be rid of such abuse,

she swiftly pressed the delete button for all incoming messages, switched it off and, with trembling fingers placed the phone on the table. His threats had reached such a high level, she was going to have to do something about it. First thing in the morning she would make a start by changing her number and notifying all her contacts.

The pleasure of the evening was now totally ruined. Rosa sighed wearily and made her way upstairs wondering if she would ever be rid of him.

★　★　★

Rosa was heading for her car when she saw Gareth coming away from the stone barn in the company of a heavy-set man who looked to be in his fifties. Their body language was relaxed, their conversation animated. This had to be Rod Griffith, she decided, wishing she felt more alert. After the shock of last night's texts she had barely slept a wink; scenarios involving Nick, which in the light of day now seemed ridiculous, had played over and over in her mind robbing her of sleep and increasing her anxiety.

'Rosa, this is Rod,' Gareth began the introduction, 'Rod . . . Rosa.'

She made an effort and raised a smile and offered her hand. 'Good to meet you,' she said.

Her smile not returned. With a nod Rod briefly gripped her hand. 'Gareth tells me we'll be working together.'

From his tone and expression she sensed he wasn't particularly enamoured of this. He went on to explain that his men had made a start on digging out the floor. After discussing a few more details both were unanimous on the amount of concrete needed and Rosa offered to order this from a firm he recommended. He then took his leave telling Gareth he was off to check on some other work he was doing and promised to see them both later that afternoon.

'Don't worry about Rod,' Gareth said as they watched him walk over to his truck and climb inside. He gave her a look of encouragement. 'Like I said, he tends to get straight to the point which can come across as a bit abrupt at times, but he does a great job and once he sees you know what you're talking about, you'll get along fine.'

'Glad to hear it,' she responded tartly. Right now she could do without men with their preconceived ideas about women's capabilities.

'Is everything okay?'

'Yes,' she emphasised a bit too forcefully, then told herself he didn't deserve to be the butt of her bad humour, especially after the wonderful time he given her the night before. 'I have to go over to Bangor but I shouldn't be long.' She had checked earlier and found a shop in the city's high street which suited her needs. 'I need a new SIM card for my mobile.'

He remembered the call she'd taken from her ex. Was he hounding her again?

'Problems with your phone?' he fished. She nodded, not wanting to go into detail. 'If I take the turn off for Bangor on the Expressway will it take me straight in to the city?'

'Not directly. Your best plan would be to take the Menai Bridge instead of the Britannia.'

'The Menai,' she repeated, 'of course.' She'd read an article about it in the local paper the other day; the accompanying photograph was impressive. 'I've been meaning to take a look.'

'I don't think you'll be disappointed. Just take the coast road; it's well signed, you can't miss it.' He gave her a thoughtful look. 'See you later?'

She nodded. 'Yes, will do.'

Following Gareth's instructions, Rosa's concentration on the trip gave her a temporary reprieve from her troubles. Even when she saw Erin's Range Rover heading in the opposite direction it didn't bother her. She guessed she was on her way to see Gareth. What he'd told her last night had put a whole new slant on things.

Rosa's spirits continued to rise as she

drove past open fields full of yet more grazing sheep and newborn lambs, on through small hamlets and villages, but what impressed her most of all was the undulating coastline, majestic in places with towering sea cliffs, in other parts with hints of welcoming golden sandy bays. What a glorious place this was!

As she checked her rear view mirror before indicating to overtake the vehicle in front, she came back down to earth with a bang. Her heart struck her ribs and her grip tightened on the wheel as she struggled to master the sense of panic threatening to overtake her. Disbelieving, she threw another glance into the mirror.

Behind her, and rapidly closing the gap between them, was Nick's red Lotus Elise convertible.

It can't be! she told herself.

His parting shot that he'd guessed where she was and his threat to expect a visit if she didn't concede to his demands returned to haunt her.

After the car in front took the next

left turn and disappeared from view, she swiftly checked her mirror again. In that fleeting glance she could just make out that, like Nick, the driver was fair-haired and appeared to be the right build, but the vehicle was too far back to clearly make out the registration number.

Another anxious look told her it was gaining on her. Her sense of panic increased. What were his intentions? The lightness of traffic in both directions was something she had been appreciating, but now brought on a sense of isolation. As the road curved and the red car momentarily disappeared from view, she considered taking the lane coming up on her left as a means of escape, but then changed her mind. From her experience Anglesey's country lanes were often deserted for miles on end.

Nick wasn't stupid. He was bound to guess what she'd done and have enough time to do the same. With no one around he could overtake and make her stop — or even worse, force her into a ditch. She was safer staying on the main road. Once she arrived in Bangor, her car securely locked, there was nothing he could do within the busy city. Then she would ring Gareth.

As the road straightened, Rosa checked her mirror again, prepared to press down on the throttle to widen the gap between them when she noticed the car had dropped back. After indicating a right turn it disappeared from view.

For a brief moment she was perplexed. Then slowly the realisation that it must have been someone else with the same model of car wrapped itself around her like a comfort blanket.

'Idiot!' she exclaimed aloud. It was all becoming clear; by making those threats Nick was playing mind games with her. Well, now she'd got the measure of him it wouldn't happen again.

All thoughts of Nick dissolved when she caught her first glimpse of Thomas Telford's magnificent suspension bridge with its impressive stone towers and graceful sweep of wrought iron cables spanning the deceptively calm surface of the Menai Strait. She recalled the article having said it was probably the most beautiful major suspension bridge in the world. *I wouldn't argue with that*, she thought as she drove onto it. In no time at all she was on the mainland and heading for Bangor's city centre.

★ ★ ★

'Gareth is over the moon you're helping with the conversion,' Betsan said. The two women were sitting in his kitchen drinking coffee after she had insisted Rosa join her when she heard her car returning. Owen and Rhys had the day off school and were outside with their uncle.

'I'm looking forward to it, too,' Rosa said. 'Most of the work on the cottage is done now, so I'll be able to give him my full attention soon.'

Betsan grinned. 'I think he'd be even more delighted if you did that.'

Rosa felt her cheeks warming. 'Purely in a business sense,' she said, giving her a wry look.

'I see . . . ' Betsan's expression changed but there was still a twinkle in her eye. 'Have you given any more thought to what you'll do when your work here is finished?'

'Yes and no,' she hedged, thinking a life on the island was just a pipe dream. 'But I'm going to have to make up my mind soon. I had to go back home a few days ago on business and it was weird. Everything felt so different, which is crazy.' She shrugged and reached for her coffee again, missing Betsan's thoughtful look.

'I always remember Mam saying home is where the heart is,' Betsan said as the kitchen door opened. 'Sounds a bit sugary but — '

'Did I hear someone mention sugar?' Gareth interrupted as he and the boys piled in. 'Hope there's something to go with it . . . tea . . . coffee?'

While his sister rolled her eyes, he smiled across at Rosa. 'Got what you wanted in Bangor?'

'Yes, it's all sorted,' she replied casually, while inside she felt like flinging herself into his arms and telling him all her troubles and about her scare on the way there.

Rhys headed straight for Rosa and asked, 'Will you come on Saturday? We need more quipment.'

Quipment? She shot a look at Betsan.

'We're having a fund-raising day at school,' she explained, 'for some new sports equipment.'

'Oh, I see,' Rosa smiled.

'For the gym,' Owen chipped in. 'We could show you our classrooms, if you like.'

'Now that would be good,' she enthused. 'I'll be able to see where you do all your hard work.'

Owen looked delighted.

She turned back to Rhys who looked as if he was waiting for an answer. 'Of course, I'll come,' she said and was touched when his face lit up. 'Will there be lots of stalls with things to buy?'

He nodded. 'And face painting and games and' — his eyes widened — 'a bouncy castle.'

'Well,' she exclaimed, 'in that case I'll definitely be there. What time does it start?'

Rhys glanced at his mother.

'Ten o'clock,' she said.

Rhys beamed. He turned to Gareth who had helped himself to coffee and was leaning against the kitchen units, mug in hand listening with some amusement to the conversation.

'Uncle Gareth, you'll have to bring her 'cos she doesn't know where our school is.'

'Hang on a minute, Rhys,' Betsan said. 'You know Uncle Gareth is very busy with the lambs.'

'Don't worry, I'll bring Rosa,' Gareth said quickly, throwing Rosa a glance, 'if she'd like me to, that is . . . '

'Of course. That would be great,'

Rosa said, forcing herself not to linger for too long within his gaze. 'And now I have some work to be getting on with. Thanks for the coffee, Betsan,' she said as she got up from the table, then turned to the boys. 'See you Saturday.'

7

'Looks like a good turn out,' Gareth said as he and Rosa approached the village school, which was decked out with colourful bunting fluttering in the breeze. Attached to the school railings a brightly painted notice obviously created by the pupils advertised the event.

Cars were parked nose to tail outside but Gareth eventually found a parking place on the opposite side some distance away. As they waited to cross the road, he took Rosa's hand before they attempted to make their way through the gaps in the heavy traffic coming both ways.

Rosa welcomed his gesture. His grip felt strong and firm — and safe. For a moment she reflected on the frightening texts she'd received and her scare the other day on her way to Bangor. But now that she'd worked out Nick's strategy and she was coping there was no need, she felt, to involve Gareth.

'Ready for it?' He grinned down at her a few moments later as he ushered her inside.

'Of course,' she smiled.

'OK, brace yourself,' he warned. As soon as he opened the door to the assembly hall, the volume of noise was deafening.

'I did warn you,' he shouted above the racket.

'You did,' she shouted back, her eyes sparkling with enjoyment. 'Let's go and find the boys.'

Once inside the crowded hall, she could see tables had been set up around its perimeter, selling everything under the sun.

'Betsan's over there,' he nodded. With the advantage of his height he had a much clearer view above the crowds than Rosa had. He took her hand again and a tiny shiver of pleasure ran through her. It felt so right.

'Don't want to lose you amongst this

lot,' he said as they began to squeeze their way through.

'You made it!' Betsan beamed from behind an attractively arranged table laden with home-made cakes and pastries. Rosa was aware that Betsan had noticed she and Gareth were holding hands.

Not wanting her to get the wrong idea, she slipped from his hold and rooted through her bag for her purse. 'I must buy some of these,' she said, 'before they all go.'

'Anything for you, Gareth?' Betsan asked after he and Rosa had moved to one side while she served several other customers.

He scratched his head for a moment. 'That crusty looks good.' He pointed. 'You know what I like. Where are the boys and Huw?'

'Further up the hall. Having their faces painted — just the boys, that is,' she grinned, 'not Huw.'

Betsan picked up the plastic carriers she'd filled for them both and placed them on a chair behind her. 'You'd best leave these here while you take a look around. I don't think they'd survive this crowd.'

'Make sure you don't sell them again,' Gareth teased before they turned to move on.

'As if,' she replied, giving him a pained look.

Their progress was slow as he kept being waylaid by people he knew. After being introduced to yet another of his old school friends and the conversation turning to the latest faming methods, Rosa's gaze began to wander. Then she saw a stall selling books near where they were standing and her interest was sparked.

She touched Gareth's arm to get his attention. 'I'm just going to take a look at the book stall.' She pointed towards it.

'OK,' he smiled back. 'I'll catch up with you in a minute.'

Rosa was soon in her element searching through the hundreds of books for sale. She pounced quickly on several titles by some of her favourite crime writers, then began to browse through the rest.

Distracted by hearing someone calling out Gareth's name, her heart sank when she realised who it was. She looked over just in time to see Erin plant an enthusiastic kiss on his cheek. As he shot a glance in her direction, his pained expression brought a smile to her face. She wondered if the expensively suited older man accompanying her was Erin's father. She had her answer when she heard Gareth greet him.

On first impressions, Rosa didn't take to Henry Martin's loud tone, his florid complexion and air of self-importance. She could clearly hear him bragging that, as head of the school's board of governors, he felt it was his duty to always give his full support to events like these.

'And have you given any more thought to my offer on the barn?' he added just as loudly.

Rosa cringed at the man's lack of tact. Gareth's expression immediately darkened. She held her breath, wondering how he would respond.

'I'm taking a break from business right now,' she heard him say. 'We're here for the children.'

'Of course, of course,' Henry Martin blustered. 'But a successful business-man never takes time off, you know, although it might appear so.'

'Maybe,' Gareth said, still looking as if he was keeping his anger under control. 'You'll have to excuse me.' He glanced in Rosa's direction. 'I think Rosa has finished at the book stall.'

Erin spun round, her face like thunder. 'Oh, so she's tagged along, too,' she heard her retort.

'I invited her,' Gareth said coldly. 'And I'm pleased to say she accepted.'

With that, he made his way to where she was standing. He still looked irritated.

'Sorry about that.' He sighed. 'Erin's

being Erin again.'

She shrugged.

'D'you know, I almost feel sorry for her. With a personality like hers she can't have much fun.'

He gave her a wry look.

'Only when she's getting her own way and then she's ecstatic — until she wants something else. Found anything of interest?'

'One or two,' she smiled.

His brows rose when she turned to lift two filled carriers off the table. 'Look's like you do a lot of reading.'

She laughed. 'I tend to, and I can never pass up a bargain where books are concerned.'

'Let me take them for you,' he offered. 'Is there anything else you want to look at or should we see if we can find the boys?'

'The boys!' she exclaimed. 'They might be wondering where we are and I want to treat them before all this is over.'

Moments later as they headed back to Betsan's stall, she heard Owen shout excitedly, 'There she is — there's Rosa.'

Betsan and a man she took to be Huw were sitting behind the now almost empty table drinking cups of tea. Both boys, their faces painted, were tucking into blueberry muffins.

Gareth greeted his brother-in-law and attempted to introduce Rosa to him while Owen grabbed hold of his free arm and Rhys grabbed Rosa's hand.

Liking Huw on sight and pretending not to recognise the boys in their face paint, she said, 'Didn't you bring Owen and Rhys after all? I can't see them anywhere.'

'We're here, we're here!' Rhys shouted, jumping up and down while Owen had a broad smile on his face. 'I'm a tiger,' Rhys continued to shout, 'and Owen's a lion.'

Rosa bent down and gave them a closer look then exclaimed, 'I don't believe it — it is you! Well, that's the best face painting I've ever seen. Don't you think so, Gareth?' She shot him a smile.

'I certainly do,' he said, pretending to look amazed too.

'You can have yours painted, too,' Rhys said at the top of his voice. 'And you Uncle Gareth. Come on.'

This brought a chorus of laughter from several people standing nearby and someone called out, 'Go on Gareth.'

'Maybe next time, eh?' Rosa suggested diplomatically. Gareth just had time to deposit her books on the table as both boys began to pull them away from it.

'Remember you said you'd show us around and don't forget,' she added, 'I've got to see your classrooms before we leave.'

That did the trick, and with that they were dragged away in the opposite direction to see more of what was on offer.

'I think we've done just about everything now,' Gareth said later after they had treated the boys to turns on the games stalls, a session on the bouncy castle and accompanied them on the miniature railway set up on the school's playing field. 'It's time we headed back inside. Your mum and dad will be wondering where you are.'

'OK,' Owen said. With that he shot off towards the rear entrance with Rhys racing after him. 'I'll go and tell them we've finished,' he called back.

'Will they be alright?' Rosa asked anxiously, as they disappeared from her line of sight. People were drifting away now and she was concerned they might follow the crowds around the side of the building and out onto the front.

'They're fine.' Gareth took her hand again where the field sloped down onto the pathway circulating the building. 'I was watching them all the way. They've just disappeared inside.'

'Good,' she said.

'Fancy a pub lunch before we go back? We could go to the one I mentioned the other night.'

His reminder of her trip home immediately cast a shadow over her mood but then she brightened again. 'That would be lovely,' she agreed after a pause that had him wondering what was wrong.

They rejoined Betsan, Huw and the boys in the hall where people were making a start on clearing things away.

'Thanks for coming,' Betsan said to Rosa. 'It meant a lot to Owen and Rhys. They've been talking about seeing you again for most of the week, you know.'

Rosa was touched. 'It's been great,' she enthused. 'I enjoyed every minute.' Despite, she reflected, Erin's constant background scrutiny as they had made their way around the stalls.

'Perhaps you and Gareth could come over for a barbeque some time,' Betsan suggested. 'Once the weather picks up a bit more and he's not so busy. Easter can be really warm here sometimes. Fingers crossed for this year.'

'Love to,' Rosa said — and suddenly realised that acknowledging their pairing was beginning to feel somehow . . . well just right.

* * *

A short drive later, they were settled in a cosy corner of the old inn, away from the main heat of a blazing open fire set in a wide stone hearth. Rosa looked around the room, admiring the thick whitewashed walls hung with gleaming brasses and framed photographs of bygone sailing ships and crewmen.

'Seen anything you fancy?' Gareth asked after they had both studied a slate chalkboard fastened to the wall across from where they were sitting. It listed a variety of dishes.

'I'm spoilt for choice.' She pondered once more what was on offer and then she made up her mind. 'Right — I'll have the salmon fishcake with salad, please.'

'So that's one salmon fishcake, and sausage and mash with onion gravy for me.' He got to his feet. 'And what would you like to drink?'

'Lime and soda, please.'

'Back in a minute.' Then he was off,

bringing a smile to her face as she heard him repeatedly muttering their order to himself as he made his way over to the bar.

Moments later, he placed her drink and a pint of beer for himself down on the table between them. 'You were quick,' she said.

'Just got in before the rush.' He sat down alongside her then picked up his glass. 'Cheers,' he toasted before taking a gulp. 'Give it another ten minutes and the place will be heaving.'

He took another pull of his beer while Rosa sipped at her glass. The companionable silence began to stretch a little.

'So,' Gareth prompted, 'is the place still growing on you . . . like you said when you got back from Norfolk?' The lightness of his tone belied how much her answer would mean to him.

Rosa looked down at her glass thinking any place on earth would do, just as long as she was with him — but no way was she going to admit that to him. For a moment he had the feeling he wasn't going to like what she was about to say.

'It is,' she said. 'Especially after what happened while I was there.' It was out before she could stop herself and immediately she sensed Gareth tense. The concern furrowing his brow was all she needed to open up and tell all.

'On the business side, it couldn't have gone more smoothly,' she told him. Emma is dealing with the final winding-up and I should be hearing from her again fairly soon.'

'But?' he said quietly, capturing her eyes.

'But . . . ' She sighed. She played with the fringe of her scarf for a moment. 'Nick turned up out of the blue when I was on my way to her office.' She gave Gareth a wry look. 'It was my own fault really; I'd taken a call from him days before without checking the number.' She shook her head at her own mistake. 'And in the row that followed I was stupid enough to let slip

I was coming to see Emma.'

The tension in Gareth's expression increased and she noticed his hand form a fist.

'What happened?' he asked quietly.

Why not tell him everything? she thought — so then she did. She told him every detail, including the text messages she'd found the night they'd shared the takeaway. As she told her story, she watched his expression grow more stone-like.

'He was canny enough not to put his name to them and I didn't recognise the number,' she added. 'But who else could be that vindictive?'

The publican arrived with their food, causing a minor distraction.

'That's why I went over to Bangor on Monday morning to change my SIM card,' she continued once they were alone again. 'On the drive there I thought I saw his car — it's quite distinctive.' Then she brushed this off with a shrug. 'But that was just me being paranoid. Anyway, with my new number there's no way he'll ever be able to threaten me again now.'

Rosa felt so much better for telling him what had been troubling her for days. Gareth continued to look at her, making no attempt to start eating.

'Don't let it go cold.' She nodded towards his plate as she took out the knife and fork from the paper napkin alongside her own. Feeling a huge weight had been lifted from her shoulders, her appetite had returned.

'It's a pity you deleted those texts,' Gareth said, not long after they had both begun to eat.

'Why?' She frowned.

'Just in case . . . ' He broke off, not wanting to scare her. 'You're right,' he hastened. 'It's unlikely you'll ever see or hear from him again.' He picked up his glass and gave her a smile. 'And here's to that.'

She responded in kind. 'Definitely. So let's forget about it. From now on I'm determined to stay focused on what's ahead of me and not dwell on the past.'

As they drove out of the inn's car park later, Rosa said, 'Thanks for lunch. It was great. I can see what you meant now about the Ships Tavern. It really is something special.'

Gareth threw her a smile before turning his attention back to the road. 'In that case we'll have to do it again — soon.'

'OK,' she chuckled, delighted with his suggestion.

She was glad his attention was taken with the traffic. The sense of security she'd gained from seeing the depths of his concern for her when she'd talked about Nick was still warming her inside. She wanted to reach out and kiss him.

Even the appearance of Erin's Range Rover taking the turn off for Llangefni in the opposite direction from where they were coming didn't dampen her spirits. As Gareth made no mention of it, she wondered if he'd seen her, too.

'Back to work,' he said after they had both got out of the Land Rover and he'd carried in the two bags of books for her while she held the bags of goodies they had both bought.

'Afraid so,' she said, handing him his. 'I need to catch up on some chores.'

'I'll see you later?' He raised a brow.

'How about dinner?' she smiled. 'With Betsan's apple tart or carrot cake to finish?'

His grin was answer enough.

'Seven o'clock again?'

Warm happiness coursed through her when he said, 'I'll see you then.'

After he had left, whistling cheerfully as he crossed the yard, Rosa turned her attention to what needed to be done.

She began to empty the plastic carriers, placing the apple tart in the fridge and the cake in one of Nina's storage containers. After turning her attention to the books she'd bought, she resisted the urge to browse through them, or any minute now she'd find herself with her nose in one and nothing would get done. She had other things to see to — most importantly of all, a meal to plan for that evening.

After loading the washing machine and tidying up around the house a little, she remembered the kitchen bin needed emptying. She pushed up the sleeves of her sweater, removed the lid and pulled out the bulging liner. Happily thinking of Gareth and the time they'd just spent together, she stepped into the yard and walked around to the side of the cottage where the wheelie bins were stored not far from where she parked.

Rosa stopped short, the bag falling from her hand. Feeling the breath leave her body she staggered back against the cottage wall, frozen to the spot and utterly disbelieving of what she was seeing . . .

Just yards away from where she stood, the cheerful cherry-red bodywork of her car was now viciously scarred. Crude ugly circles were burnt into the paint-work, across the roof, down to the bonnet and across the doors, exposing the bare metal on every panel.

With sickening effect came the realisation that Nick's threats were real after all. It must have been his car she'd seen the day she drove to Bangor. It was pure luck she'd been able to keep enough distance between them for him not to recognise her registration number at the time.

Despite what she, Nina and Paul had all thought, he had remembered the village . . . the cottage — and rightly guessed that this was where she was. Her heart thundered against her ribs; he could still be here.

Panic overtook Rosa. Any moment she expected to see him appear from around the front of the cottage and come bearing down on her.

With her gaze fixed on the end of the wall and the boundary between the farm and the lane beyond it, she backed away until her trembling fingers felt the rear corner of the building. Taking a deep breath, she turned and ran towards the farmhouse, desperately calling out for Gareth.

The back door was yanked open before she reached it and he came hurrying outside. With her breathing now coming in sobs, she flung herself at him.

'What the — ?' she heard him exclaim as she gripped his sweater and buried her head against his chest.

Gareth quickly curved his arms around her protectively as she held on tightly to him.

'Rosa, calm down . . . it's OK,' he soothed.

She felt the warmth of his hand as he softly brushed her head and continued to hold her to him until he sensed she was gradually overcoming whatever it was that had scared her.

'Come inside and tell me what's wrong,' he said. With one arm around her shoulders he guided her into the kitchen and led her to the armchair. Once she was seated he hunkered down in front of her, his brow deeply furrowed, his eyes full of concern as she rubbed her upper arms and stared vacantly into space.

'Rosa?' he prompted softly.

She gave him such a look of desperation he wanted to take hold of her again, assure her she would always be safe with him.

She swallowed against the dryness in her throat and said in little more than a whisper, 'He's here. Nick's here.'

'What? Where?' Gareth shot to his feet. 'Don't tell me he's in the cottage.'

She shivered, then shook her head.

'No, but my car . . . it's wrecked.'

For a few moments he considered what she'd said and tried to make sense of it. Then he put his hand on her shoulder. When she looked back up at him, the fear in her eyes twisted like a knife.

'I want you to stay right there; you're quite safe, understand?'

She nodded silently.

'I'll take a look. I won't be a minute. OK?'

'OK,' she repeated shakily.

As he was about to turn away, she

reached out for his hand. Eyes wide with anxiety, she looked up at him. 'Please be careful. He might still be here somewhere.'

His look of assurance calmed her fears. 'I shouldn't think so, but if he is, don't worry. There's no way he'd ever get the better of me.'

Despite Gareth's reassurances, it felt like an eternity before he walked back into the house. The cat shot in ahead of him, aiming straight for where Rosa sat. She could tell from his expression that what he'd seen had shocked him.

'I'll make some tea,' was all he said.

While he reached for the kettle, the cat jumped up onto her lap, mewing for attention.

'Hello, miss,' Rosa said softly, pleased to have her there. After performing a few unsteady circles, the animal settled down and began to purr. Rosa stroked her small head, the purring having a therapeutic effect on her while she watched Gareth move around the kitchen.

Eventually he came over and offered her a mug of steaming tea.

'Drink this,' he said. 'I've put plenty of sugar in. It's supposed to help with shock.'

'Thanks.' She took it from him.

He continued to look down at her, concern still etched on his face. 'Are you warm enough? I can get a blanket or something for you.'

'No, I'm fine.' She gave him a wan smile and then glanced down at the cat. 'She's just like a hot water bottle.'

'If you're sure?' He pulled out a chair from under the table and drew it up close to the armchair beside her.

Silence reigned for a few moments while she sipped her tea and suppressed a shudder; she knew he meant well, but it tasted like syrup.

'I doubt it was him,' he said out of the blue. 'No — think about it,' he added as she was about to protest. 'From what you told me earlier, you and Nina and Paul were convinced he wouldn't remember where the cottage is. If the idea of you being here had crossed his mind, would he seriously consider travelling all this way, not knowing for sure where you were staying, and yet somehow manage to pinpoint the exact spot? This is a big island.'

Rosa considered what he'd just said, desperately wanting him to be right, but Nick's threats still echoed in her mind.

'Mindless vandalism is everywhere,' Gareth broke into her thoughts. 'And there's no exception, not even here. Where you park, the boundary wall is at its lowest and your car is clearly visible from the lane. Any idiot so minded could hop over and back again in a matter of minutes.'

'But why pick someone at random to do that to?'

He shrugged. 'Beats me. Who knows what goes on in some people's heads? But it's the only logical answer. Don't worry — they'll be long gone by now.'

She sighed, taking some reassurance from his explanation. 'I suppose it makes more sense. It must have been the shock giving me these crazy ideas.' But still she gave him a worried look. 'I just hope you're right.'

He got to his feet and gave her a smile of encouragement. 'I bet you it'll turn out that way. I'll get on to the police, though, as it still has to be reported — and you'll need to contact your insurance company.'

'Yes, of course,' she said. 'Their number's listed in my phone but the policy documents are back at my parents' house with a lot of other paperwork and stuff.'

'Once you've explained the situation I'm sure the insurers will sort it for you.'

'But my phone's still in my bag,' she said.

'Would you like me to get it for you?' Despite her coming round to his way of thinking, Gareth sensed she was still feeling anxious.

'Do you mind?'

'Of course not.' He smiled. 'Stay

there. I'll be back in a second.'

With Gareth being so strongly supportive, gradually Rosa began to feel a whole lot better.

★ ★ ★

Gareth popped his head around the kitchen door. 'The police are here,' he called.

Rosa came to with a start. She had readily taken up his invitation to stay in the farmhouse while he was over in the sheds and, with the cat asleep on her lap, it hadn't been too long before she had drifted off, too. She carefully eased up from the chair and deposited the protesting cat back upon the cushions.

'They're just pulling into the yard,' he added and waited for her to join him so they could go outside together. While she watched the two officers get out of their vehicle, Rosa braced herself to show them her car.

'You will stay while I talk to them?' she asked Gareth a little anxiously. 'I might forget something.'

'Of course I will.' He strode over to greet the two policemen while she waited not far from the house. A brief discussion in Welsh followed, then he brought them over to her.

'I hear you're the owner,' one of them said sympathetically after he'd introduced himself and his colleague.

'Yes.' She nodded.

'Let's take a look then, shall we?'

'It's this way,' Gareth indicated then took her hand before they walked down the yard.

'Nasty,' the other officer said to his colleague as they walked around the car giving it a cursory look. 'They probably used paint stripper.'

Hearing this, she was thankful she wasn't wearing her decorating overalls. For some crazy reason the thought struck her they might think she'd done it herself.

'Do you know of anyone who has a grudge against you?' he asked.

She shook her head. 'No, no one.'

She'd had time to think over what Gareth had said about the improbability of Nick being here and come to believe he was right.

'In that case it will go down as an act of vandalism. Have you contacted your insurance company yet and reported the damage?'

'No.' She shook her head. 'I was waiting for you to take a look at it first.'

'Fair enough,' he nodded. He took out a pad. 'This is the report number you'll need for them.' He gave her a sympathetic smile as he handed it to her. 'Let's hope a courtesy car is included in your policy because this one's going nowhere except on a pick-up truck. If we do trace the culprits — and there's usually more than one in cases like these — we'll get back to you. Otherwise there's nothing much else we can do. Your insurer will take over once you've been in touch.'

After a few more words in Welsh to Gareth and a shaking of hands all round, they left.

'Apparently there have been a few incidents across the island lately, according to what the officers just told me,' he said as they stood and watched them drive away. He gave her a look of sympathy. 'It's just your bad luck to be another victim. How are you feeling now?'

She shrugged, feeling a little foolish that her initial reactions had been a bit over the top.

'I'm fine, thanks to you,' she said. 'And now I'd best get on to the insurance company.'

*   *   *

That night with the events of the day replaying in her mind, it took some time before she finally drifted off to sleep — and dreamed of Nick roaming around outside the cottage trying to find a way in. Then he was there in her room, looming over her, his face contorted with anger, but she couldn't move — her body was paralysed with fear.

With a gasp she woke, heart racing,

her eyes wide to see there was no one standing there staring down at her, just empty shadows darkening the room. She reached for her phone and checked the time. It had just turned 1 am.

Knowing sleep was impossible, Rosa got out of bed and pushed her feet into her slippers. The day had deteriorated into an evening of cold, squally weather. Wind moaned in the chimney and the room felt bitterly cold. Maybe a hot milky drink would help her get back to sleep.

Then she heard a sound outside.

In this weather it could be anything, she reassured herself. Since her time at the cottage, she'd come to understand the countryside was not as quiet as she'd believed. Still she glanced across at the window, at the same time straining her ears waiting to hear if it was repeated. After the scare she'd had, believing she'd seen Nick's car, the damage done to her own car, and now the nightmare she'd just woken from, common sense was taking a back seat.

She was being irrational, she knew it, but if she didn't check to see if there was anyone outside before she went downstairs, she knew she would not leave the room.

Getting to her feet and shivering after leaving the warmth of her bed, she reached for the long woollen cardigan she'd left on top of the duvet, quickly pulled it on and then walked across to the window. Taking a breath she took hold of one of the curtains and eased it aside.

It took a few moments for her eyes to adjust to the inky darkness of the starless night. Then gradually familiar shapes began to take form: the curve of the track that led from the lane to the cottage; beyond it, pale hints of the boundary wall came into view then disappeared again behind the moving shrubbery. From what she could see of the lane there were no unfamiliar parked cars, nobody to be seen. It appeared totally deserted.

She began to relax, assuring herself

that no one in their right mind would be out on a night like this. It was time to heat some milk then get back to bed.

Just as she was about to draw the curtain again, the moon broke through the clouds revealing more of the shadowed hedgerows on the far side of the lane. From the corner of her eye she sensed there was something different about what she was seeing. Her grip tightened on the curtain as she peered out through the glass. There, among the irregular shapes and shadows the wind was creating, one dark shape remained stock-still. She blinked. Gradually the shape took on a recognisable form.

Rosa's stomach clenched. Someone was out there; she was sure of it.

* * *

'I can't believe everything is coming together so quickly and we're at the first fixings stage,' Rosa said to Rod as they both scanned the interior of the barn.

After the trauma of the previous night,

she had opened the bedroom curtains that morning to see everything looking so normal, so familiar, she doubted what she'd seen. Maybe it had been a lingering part of her nightmare or a figment of her imagination.

Either way, she decided she would make no mention of it to Gareth. Today, in the sunshine, she was determined to forget all about it.

'Yes, it's looking good.' Rod shot her a look of respect. During their regular site meetings over the last few weeks he'd come to realise his initial impression of her as being a mere slip of a girl had been turned on its head. Rosanna Ryan knew what she was talking about.

In front of them on the new concrete floor, the interior walls separating the two lets had been erected. Now it was a hive of activity as electricians and plumbers tackled their work.

Just then her mobile rang and Rosa frowned, wondering when she would be able to pick up without worrying who it might be.

'I'll leave you to it,' Rod said while she reached inside her jeans pocket. 'See you later.'

'Yes, of course. Thanks, Rod.'

He walked away and began a conversation with one of the men.

The number displayed on the screen was new to her. She took a breath and answered, relaxing again when it turned out to be the garage who was supplying her with a courtesy car until her insurance claim was settled. She confirmed her present address and that she was there to accept delivery as soon as possible.

★ ★ ★

'So how are things?'

'Couldn't be better.' Rosa responded happily to Nina's question, cheered to hear her voice. 'Everything's coming along really well in the cottage and on the conversion.'

'That's great, but really I meant with you.'

'Oh, I'm OK . . . enjoying the work, the island, the weather . . . ' She'd held back on telling her about the vandalism. She knew it would only bother her. It could wait until she and Paul arrived at the end of the week and saw she had a different car.

'Strange there's no mention of Gareth there. Don't tell me you two have fallen out.'

Rosa rolled her eyes. 'Of course not. We're two very busy people, that's all . . . ships that pass in the night and all that.'

'But it must be sort of lonely for the two of you just working all the time.'

'We take a break now and again,' she protested. 'Remember me telling you we were at his nephews' fund-raising event? And we've had lunch together once or twice. And I've cooked dinner for us both a few times. We can't be in each other's pockets every minute of the day, as much as you'd like us to.'

'What — me? I never said a word.'

'Not directly, no.' Rosa laughed. 'But

I've known you long enough to be able to guess how your mind works.'

'You have to admit though, he is a great catch,' Nina said outright.

Rosa could sense the eagerness in Nina's tone. 'I suppose he is but you well know men are off my agenda just now.'

Liar, her inner voice said emphatically.

'But you can't go on like that forever. They're not all like Nick, you know.'

Rosa closed her eyes. *Don't go there again*, she pleaded silently, her worries of his threats coming to the fore again.

'Sorry,' Nina hastened. 'I didn't mean to mention him. It just came out. From what I've heard since you were here, he appears to be lying low. No one's seen him lately which I suppose is understandable. He probably realises just how close he was to having the police knocking on his door. Anyway, let's change the subject.'

No one's seen him lately?

Long after she had ended the call,

237

Nina's comment repeated itself over and over in the back of her mind.

A sudden wave of nausea churned her stomach. It was too much of a coincidence. If no one had seen him around her home town, then he must be here on the island after all and had somehow traced her to the farm.

She'd been right all along!

Ruining her car was just the start — and if that had been him in the lane last night, what would happen next?

She needed to unburden her troubles, to tell Gareth what she'd seen and what she'd just learned from Nina, but would he believe her?

He was so convinced vandals had caused the car damage that he would probably just say her mind was playing tricks on her. Besides, he had his own concerns to deal with right now and the last thing he needed was to become embroiled in her problems.

All she could do was to take each day as it came and deal with whatever it brought.

8

The joists had been fitted for the upper floors and they were now aligning the first staircase into place. As he looked around and took in the progress that was being made, Gareth exclaimed above the constant echoing rhythm of the joiners' hammering, 'This is great!'

He glanced down at Rosa, his expression full of pleasure. 'It's really taking shape.' Then he sobered a little. 'I just hope the bank manager is of the same opinion,' he added as they left the men to their work and walked back to the yard.

She could sense a sudden air of apprehension about him; he'd told her earlier he had another appointment to discuss extending his loan.

'Why not suggest he come and take a look?' she said. 'Once he sees how well the conversion is going he's bound to look favourably on it.'

Gareth slapped his forehead with the palm of his hand, making Rosa laugh. 'Now why didn't I think of that?'

'He might be planning on doing so anyway,' she said. 'It's happened a few times with other projects I've worked on.' She hesitated, not sure of how he would take what she was going to suggest, but then she went for it. 'If it should turn out that there is a problem I'd like to help out. The money has come through from Emma and — '

He held up his hand, cutting her short.

'No, Rosa,' he said firmly. 'Definitely not. I can't take your money. You'll need it yourself to get started again. End of.'

Her brows rose and she threw him a wry look. This man was so proud.

'What I was going to say, if you'd let me finish, was it's a lot more than I'd expected; more than enough for my needs.'

'No.' He was emphatic. 'I appreciate

what you're saying but I have to do this myself.' His manner was so intense, she wished she hadn't offered. He checked his watch. 'And I'd best get going. I'm due to see him in half an hour.'

'I'll leave you to it then,' she said, feeling slightly put out. 'Good luck.'

'Thanks. See you later.'

He headed for the farmhouse and, deflated, Rosa headed for the cottage where she took out her frustration with Gareth by putting all her energy into rubbing down a chest of drawers for the twins' bedroom in preparation for painting them a pale shade of blue.

Her mood darkened further still when she recognised the sound of Erin's vehicle roaring up the track to the farmhouse. It gave her some satisfaction to know Erin had mistimed her visit as Gareth had not long left for the bank.

Moments later, an impatient rapping on the cottage door brought a groan from Rosa and she paused in what she was doing. It could only be Erin. Should she ignore her and hope she'd go away? No — on second thoughts she was just in the mood for her . . .

Prepared for battle, Rosa yanked open the front door. Standing a short distance away from the step with not a hair out of place, Erin's expression was as poisonous as ever. She looked Rosa up and down; her distaste at seeing her wearing overalls once more was obvious.

'Have you any idea where Gareth is?' she demanded. 'I never get any sense out of that boy he employs and I need to speak to him.'

Sympathising with Ivan, who she guessed was probably terrified of Erin, Rosa decided Gareth's meeting at the bank was none of Erin's business.

'Sorry,' she said. 'I haven't a clue.'

Erin's eyes narrowed and she appeared undecided whether to believe her or not.

'I'm surprised you're still here,' she said. 'After what I heard in the village about your car I thought you'd be long gone.'

'I'm here to do a job,' Rosa replied.

'I'll see it through.' She decided she'd rattle her cage a little more. 'Besides, since that happened, Gareth's been very sympathetic and protective. He's insisted I park in the yard out of sight from the lane now so it's highly unlikely anything like that will happen again.'

Erin's eyes were like flints. 'Think you've landed on your feet, don't you? I saw the doe-eyed looks you were giving him at the school fete. Take it from me, you're wasting your time. He only brought you along because he just feels sorry for you being stuck out here on your own. Sometimes he can be too kind for his own good. And believe me, I know him better than anyone.'

The implication in her expression spelled out her meaning in foot-high letters.

'Oh, and don't use me as an excuse to call round to see him,' she added. 'I'll call him later.' With that parting shot, she turned on her heels and strode back to her car.

For a few moments Rosa stared after

Erin. She couldn't believe her cheek in issuing instructions as though she was some kind of lackey.

Deep in thought, she closed the door and went to make herself a mug of coffee. As she waited for the kettle to boil she wished she had responded with some equally cutting remark, but that would mean lowing herself to Erin's level of vindictiveness. Still, the woman's outburst continued to nag and Rosa began to second-guess herself, wondering if she'd misread the situation between herself and Gareth. He now knew most of the reasons for her failed relationship with Nick. Was his friendliness really down to him just feeling sorry for her?

Heaven forbid he had discussed her with Erin! He couldn't have, Rosa decided. If she had any idea of what she'd been through, she was bound to have brought it up in one of her tirades.

She sighed, her thoughts full of him. It was a fact — she was useless, absolutely useless when it came to judging the opposite sex.

Maybe it was time she closed the door on the fantasies she'd been creating around him and thoughts of relocating to the island. She needed to get back into the real world. Thank Heaven he had little inkling, if any, of her growing feelings for him. From now on she would have to stay focused on her work and nothing else.

★ ★ ★

At the sound of a light knocking on the kitchen door, Rosa glanced up from the papers spread out in front of her. Despite her earlier intentions, her heart still flipped when Gareth put his head around it.

'Got a minute?' He looked elated and she guessed his meeting at the bank had gone well.

'How about a coffee or, judging by your expression, maybe something stronger?' she said, getting to her feet to fill the kettle.

'Is it that obvious?' His smile spread to his eyes as he walked inside.

Then when the space between them had narrowed to mere inches, in one swift movement he produced a large bouquet from behind his back and offered it to her.

Her eyes widened as she looked at the beautiful arrangement of colourful flowers. 'What's this for?' she asked, slightly puzzled.

'For being so ungrateful about your offer. I didn't mean to be so abrupt.'

She gave him a steady look. 'Well you were.' She decided to let him suffer a little longer but when the shine went out of his eyes, her intentions dissolved and she smiled. 'But it's forgotten. You were stressed. It happens.'

He bounced back, and to her utter surprise, grabbed her by the waist and swung her around.

'The flowers!' she protested happily, while with her free hand she grabbed his shoulder for support. 'You'll crush them.'

Laughing, he set her on her feet again, his arm still around her waist as they both peered into the brown paper wrapping. 'They're fine,' he said.

'More than fine,' she said softly, glancing back up at him. 'They're beautiful.'

'Just like you . . . '

His whispered words sent her heart crashing and the raw longing in his eyes changed the atmosphere entirely.

'I'd best put them in water.'

Why had her voice become so husky? She could give him a peck on the cheek, surely? Just a thank you for bringing her such lovely flowers. That would be OK, just a friendly gesture . . . but the longer her eyes stayed locked with his, the harder it was for her to move.

As she stretched up a little to meet his cheek he turned his head slightly and her direction changed. His lips found hers, tentatively at first until their longing for each other moulded their bodies together and the flowers were in danger of being crushed beyond saving.

Held firmly within his embrace, their lips hungrily pressed together, she was aware of him taking the bouquet and placing it down on the table. As his kiss deepened, she was drawn to a place where nothing else mattered. She raised her hand and buried her fingers within the thickness of his dark hair, thrilling at its strong wiry texture.

Lost to her senses, she tried to ignore a small voice of warning, but it refused to go away. If he was just using her, she knew she wouldn't survive it. She came down to earth and pulled back her head from him.

'No, Gareth . . . I can't.'

She felt his body slump before he released her. 'Can't what?' he demanded, his expression a mixture of anger and confusion. 'I wasn't about to carry you upstairs.'

Rosa's cheeks flamed and she wished the ground would swallow her up.

Glancing away, he raked his hair with his hand. 'Sorry. I thought we had something . . . ' Then he looked back at her and shrugged. 'I can see now I got it wrong.'

'Gareth . . . ,'

She was about to say she felt exactly the same but with the memory of what Erin had said earlier still hanging over her, she just couldn't bring herself to do so.

He studied her for a moment, waiting for her to say something more, but she looked away.

'Don't you think it's about time you let go of the past?' he demanded harshly. 'Or are you going to let that ex of yours dominate your life for ever? I'm sure he'd be thrilled at the idea.'

That hit home and when she looked back at him his expression immediately softened; his anger gone.

'You need to move on, Rosa,' he said softly. 'Don't let him win out in the end.'

Should she tell him now of her fears that Nick was still intent on doing her harm? That when she left the farm, she automatically tensed at the first sight of every red car, every fair-haired man she came across; seeing him everywhere. That she'd also taken to double checking both entrance doors to the cottage were firmly locked and bolted when she was working upstairs; repeating the routine before she went to bed, only to wake at the slightest sound believing, for all her efforts, he had somehow got inside the cottage.

As he took in her strained expression, the thought suddenly struck Gareth like a hammer blow. Maybe it was him — perhaps Rosa just didn't fancy him and was too polite to say so?

Although her responses to his kiss told him something else. Damn, his mind was in a muddle.

Yet now wasn't the time for further talk. Emotions were running too high.

'I'd best get back to work,' he said and turned away.

In something of a daze Rosa watched as he quietly closed the door behind him. She glanced at the bouquet lying on the table, its brown wrapping paper slightly creased, and tears sprang to her eyes. Rubbing them away with the back of her hand, she walked over to the dresser to find the vase she'd remembered seeing inside one of the bottom cupboards.

As she stood at the sink holding it under the tap, she saw him striding across the yard to the sheds. What he'd said about letting go of the past made sense, she wouldn't argue with that. His comment about Nick winning out in the end set her thinking.

She needed to clear the air. Should she tell him what she believed she'd seen on those two occasions? What she'd recently learned from Nina had strengthened that belief, but still she hesitated . . . Mentioning it might convince Gareth that Nick was still there in her mind and always would be.

*   *   *

Two days later, Rosa had grown more miserable with every passing hour after

Gareth had made no attempt to seek her out. *He's given you up as a bad job,* she decided, *and you've only yourself to blame.* But there was no putting it off any longer. Nina and Paul would be arriving at the weekend and she needed to discuss her sleeping arrangements with him.

She had heard his back door slam a short time ago and as there was no sign of him in the yard or the open barn, she guessed he'd gone in rather than come out.

Rosa braced herself before knocking on the back door of the farmhouse. Nothing. She knocked again. Hanging around, waiting for him to answer was making her tense.

'Just get on with it,' she muttered to herself and stepped into the utility area just as he came out from the kitchen.

They both jumped like scalded cats and that broke the ice, making them both laugh, and when he looked so pleased to see her, she felt like telling him she was sorry about the other day and how much she'd missed him. Instead she said, 'How are things?'

'Fine, things are slowing down now.'

'I'd noticed the fields were filling up with new mums,' she smiled. 'The lambs are adorable.'

He gave her a look that spoke volumes, but she ignored it. They might be his livelihood but they were still cute.

'Nina and Paul will be here on Saturday and I was wondering . . . ' She hesitated. Maybe now the offer was off.

'About your room,' he finished for her. She relaxed again. 'Come and take a look now if it suits. Betsan's old room will be the best one for you.'

'She won't mind?'

He shot her a puzzled look. 'Why would she mind? Quite the opposite; she'd be delighted. I'll take you up,' he said, indicating the way.

Upstairs a central corridor divided the four bedrooms and once more she could see what potential the house had as a family home and what she could make of it, given half the chance.

'The bathroom's at the end, and next to it is the airing cupboard,' he said. 'There's a ton of spare bedding and towels, so just help yourself and there's always plenty of hot water.'

'Thanks,' she said, thinking again of how much his life must have changed since losing his parents and his sister had left home.

'This was Betsan's.' He opened the door nearest to where they were standing. 'I'm further up on the other side.'

She stepped inside and Gareth followed.

Despite the outdated floral wallpaper and slightly tired pink and cream décor, Rosa felt at home straight away. The single bed looked comfortable and the wardrobe and small dressing table would be useful. There was another stunning view over the lambing sheds into the fields and the coastline beyond.

'Lovely. I'll make a start on moving in then,' she said, turning her attention back to Gareth.

His eyes narrowed slightly as he appeared to find something of great interest in the landscape.

'Good,' was all he said.

9

The twins threatened to send Rosa flying as they both launched themselves at her. 'Aunty Rosa, Aunty Rosa!'

'We're here!' Eva shouted.

'I can see that,' Rosa laughed, pausing for breath before giving them a kiss. 'I've been looking out of the bedroom window waiting to see Daddy's car and then in the distance I saw a flash of blue . . .'

'And it was us,' Chloe shouted loudly.

'Chloe, Eva! Calm down,' Nina said, rolling her eyes as she walked up to Rosa. They hugged tightly and exchanged kisses. 'They've been fizzing since we crossed the bridge.'

'Hi, Rosa.' Paul came round from the driver's side of his dark blue BMW to greet her with a kiss on the cheek. He looked thoroughly pleased with himself.

'We made good time despite the Easter traffic.'

'Good to see you, Paul.' Full of smiles, she kissed him back. 'No doubt you're ready for a cup of tea.'

'Lead me to it,' he sighed, placing his hands on the small of his back and stretching.

As they all piled in through the front door, Nina glanced around the hall and for once was speechless.

'Are we in the right place?' Paul asked, pausing to take in the changes Rosa had made.

'It's fantastic,' Nina exclaimed. 'It looks so fresh and new — and the cream walls . . . ' Face alight, she threw Rosa a look. 'If this is anything to go on, I can't wait to see the rest.'

'Go and explore,' she suggested happily, 'while I make the tea.'

As Rosa busied herself in the kitchen, above her she could just make out the excited chatter of the twins as they discovered their new room.

'They love it so much, they won't

come down,' Nina said a short time later when she and Paul joined Rosa in the kitchen. 'And ours is just perfect, too, isn't it Paul?'

'Cracking job,' he said. 'Any time you want a break here, just say the word and it's yours. I'll make a start on bringing in the cases while the tea's brewing.'

'Need a hand?' Nina asked.

'No. It's fine. No doubt you two have got a million things to talk about since yesterday.'

Chuckling as Nina made a face at him, Paul left them to it.

'So how's Gareth?' she asked as Rosa began to line up three mugs on the counter near to the teapot.

'He's well. Not quite so busy now with most of the lambing over.'

'It will be good to see him again. I take it you're still going to sleep with him in the farmhouse while we're here.'

'Nina!' Rosa tried unsuccessfully to keep a straight face.

'What?' Nina asked, putting on an exaggerated air of innocence.

'You know exactly what. For the record, I'm using Betsan's old room.'

'Of course you are. Gareth's not involved with anyone, is he?' Nina asked, suddenly out of the blue. 'We didn't get to know everything about him when we were buying the cottage.'

Rosa recalled what he'd said about Erin. 'As far as I know, he isn't.' She frowned. 'Why?'

'And you're trying to tell me there's not been a spark of anything between you two?'

She shrugged and looked away, annoyed to feel her cheeks warming. 'I don't think I'm ready yet, Nina,' she muttered.

Her friend moved closer and put her arm around her shoulder, giving her a quick hug.

'It's time to move on,' she said. Her expression became serious. 'You mustn't let what that . . . that, I won't say it in case the children hear but you know what I mean. No way can he dictate your future.'

Rosa gave her a watery smile.

'Funny,' she said, 'Gareth said something very similar only a few days ago.'

Nina's radar picked up immediately.

'Oh, yes. Why was that?'

She could have kicked herself.

'I'll tell you later,' she hedged. 'This tea must be about stewed by now.'

'I'll pour while you talk,' Nina insisted, determined not to let her off the hook, but then Paul poked his head around the door frame.

'Is there enough tea for one more? Gareth saw the car and offered to give me a hand to bring in the last of the stuff.'

'Of course,' Nina exclaimed enthusiastically. She glanced at Rosa. 'Funny . . . we were just talking about him, weren't we?'

★　★　★

'I think a toast is in order, don't you?' Paul suggested later that evening. He

260

picked up his wineglass. 'To the chef,' he said.

Nina and Gareth raised their glasses, too.

'And cheers to you all for enjoying it so much,' Rosa responded, happily. 'I can't take credit for the tiramisu, though. That came courtesy of Carys's freezer.'

Earlier that morning before the family had arrived, she had taken her courage in both hands and driven up to the village to shop for the first time since the incident with her car, telling herself she was being ridiculous thinking she would bump into Nick. There had been a few heart-stopping moments when she'd been on the road and thought she'd seen him but had quickly realised her mistake. She had shopped at the convenience store and, driving back, congratulated herself on being right.

Back at the cottage, feeling content, she set to and prepared a lasagne to save Nina the bother of having to cook after their long drive. All she would have to do was to reheat it, put the accompanying garlic bread in the oven and make up a salad.

When Nina had spotted the foil-covered dish on the counter while making a second pot of tea and asked what it was, she had insisted Rosa and Gareth share it with them.

Now while the two men talked farming and Nina was preparing a cheese board, Rosa sipped her wine and became lost in her thoughts.

It had seemed so right, so comfortable, when she and Gareth had returned to the farmhouse to get ready for the evening. He'd insisted she use the shower first and give him a shout when she'd finished — which she did after padding along the corridor wrapped tightly in her bathrobe, hair secure in a soft white towel, to call down to him from the landing.

Later when she was ready, he'd told her she'd looked particularly gorgeous.

'You don't look half bad yourself,' she'd said, basking in his compliment.

He did look gorgeous, too, in a pale blue shirt open at the neck revealing a hint of dark chest hair.

Her thoughts were broken when Nina plonked herself back down at the table and invited them all to help themselves to cheese and biscuits.

While the two men did just that Rosa asked, 'So any plans while you're here?'

'Oh, just the usual,' Nina said. 'Weather permitting, spend as much time as we can on the beach keeping the girls entertained and just chilling out. I expect you'll be busy with the barn.'

Hearing mention of the conversion, Gareth said, 'You'll have to come and take a look. It's really taking shape. Rod tells me Rosa's had the whip out, making sure they all keep to schedule.' Briefly his eyes captured hers. 'I think he's a bit in awe of her.'

Rosa made a small sound of derision. 'I don't believe that for a minute. Rod knows exactly what he's doing. It's a team effort, that's all.'

'She's never been able to take a compliment,' Nina chipped in affectionately.

'I've figured that one out, too,' Gareth joked. 'She doesn't seem to have a particularly high opinion of herself.'

Something in the atmosphere changed and Paul came to the rescue as he shot Nina a look. 'Whereas someone not a million miles from here . . .'

'What!' Nina exclaimed. 'What are you saying?'

'Nothing,' Paul chuckled. 'Just remembering the angel costumes you made for Chloe and Eva's first nativity last Christmas. You were so proud you wanted to show the whole town.'

She pulled a face at her husband. 'I spent hours on them,' she protested. 'Besides, they looked so cute.'

'They did,' he agreed, trying to keep a straight face and failing. 'But all that glitter you doused them in . . .'

'I remember,' Rosa began to giggle. 'They lit the school stage. You should have supplied sunglasses with them.'

'They did look more like the fairy on the Christmas tree, didn't they,' Nina grinned. 'And it took ages to wash out of their hair.'

'And the furniture and the carpets,' Paul added, wryly. 'Not to mention their bedding . . . '

Laughter echoed around the table.

Rosa looked across at Gareth; happy to see him so relaxed, as if he'd known Nina and Paul for as long as she had. *This is the life*, she thought, *laughter, great friends and most of all . . . you.*

The admission was there in her mind before she could stop it, but all too soon the evening came to an end.

'We'd best let you two get to bed,' she said, noticing that Paul was having trouble suppressing a persistent yawn.

After lots of thanks and several goodnight kisses, they parted on the doorstep.

'See you tomorrow,' Nina said.

'Of course. Have a good night's sleep,' Rosa added before she and Gareth turned away.

The moon was bright, once more lighting the yard and outbuildings, and it seemed every star in the inky blackness above was on show; the only sound to be heard was an occasional muffled bleat coming from the sheds.

After Gareth opened the farmhouse door, she paused and looked up in wonder at the night sky. 'I've never seen so many stars before. It feels like I can actually reach out and touch them.'

He followed her gaze. 'I'm ashamed to say, it's something else I take for granted, but it really is spectacular. It makes you realise just how insignificant we all are in the grand scheme of things and what little time we have to get it right.'

His words struck home.

He's so right, she thought. It was time she made some decisions. Anticipation sent a slight shiver through her.

Standing so closely together, he sensed it. 'You're cold,' he said, placing his arm around her. 'Let's get you inside.'

It's not the cold, she contradicted silently. *If you only knew the real reason*.

She didn't take the thought any further. She could clearly see what she truly wanted — the man she wanted — but to take that chance, that leap?

'Care for a hot drink before we go up?'

His suggestion broke her train of thought.

'Not for me, thanks.' She smiled at him.

He nodded, then after a fraction's hesitation, said, 'I had no business saying what I did the other day. I'm sorry if I upset you.'

Rosa was surprised he'd raised the subject now.

'It's fine, it really is. I've been doing a lot of thinking and you were right.'

He moved closer to her and placed his hands on her shoulders. 'You do understand I only want what's best for you.'

She nodded. The sincerity in his

expression could not be doubted. 'Of course I do.'

'I won't crowd you, Rosa, but do you think maybe we could spend more time together?'

'Even more than this?' she joked lightly. 'I'll be living with you for the next fortnight.'

'Don't say things like that,' he joked softly, giving her such a look she had trouble concentrating on keeping things light-hearted as they shared a brief goodnight kiss.

★　★　★

Humming happily, Rosa checked the kitchen clock again then took a wholemeal loaf out of the breadbin. Gareth would be back any time now, so she might as well make a start on the sandwiches she'd promised for lunch.

Last night had been perfect — but one step at a time she told herself.

She had just begun to cut into the

loaf when a rapid knocking on the front door made her pause from what she was doing.

'I can see you're making yourself at home.'

Erin's distaste was obvious when she went and answered the door.

Rosa wondered if her own dislike was showing just as much. Wickedly, she rather hoped it was.

'When I rang before, Gareth told me you were staying here for a while,' Erin added. 'You're a fast worker. I'll give you that.'

'That's what most of my clients tell me,' Rosa clipped back.

That produced a raised eyebrow. 'So Gareth's just a client is he,' she mocked. 'Who do you think you're kidding? Believe me, you're wasting your time.'

Rosa opened her mouth to retaliate but was stopped by Erin brusquely asking where he was.

'In one of the back fields,' she said, not wishing to carry on the conversation any further. She was just about to close the door when she noticed Erin was wearing another pair of impossibly slender high heels.

'Just walk round into the yard,' she suggested. 'You might be able to see him from there.' She looked pointedly at Erin's shoes. 'If not, you can always walk across the fields. You're bound to see him eventually.'

'Oh very funny,' Erin hissed.

Then Rosa sensed the door at the other end of the hall had been opened.

From behind her she heard Gareth casually call, 'Hello, Erin. What can I do for you?'

With that, Rosa was pushed to one side as the other woman forced her way past.

'Something nice I hope,' Erin said cheerily.

Rosa couldn't believe the speed of her change of manner as she watched Gareth subtly dodge the kiss heading in the direction of his lips and ask why she was here.

Thrown slightly by his attitude, Erin

gushed, 'There's something really special I wanted to see you about. You're going to love it.'

He threw Rosa a look she couldn't decipher before he opened the sitting room door.

'You'd best come in here then.'

Despite his assurance he was not interested in Erin, a heated sense of rejection surged through Rosa as she watched the door close behind them.

Primed to take her anger out on the front door, she stopped herself from slamming it just in time; she refused to give Erin the satisfaction of getting to her. Instead, she closed it softly then walked back into the kitchen.

Disbelieving of Gareth's willing acceptance of Erin's demands, Rosa snatched up her jacket from off the back of the chair and pulled it on. No way was she going to hang around waiting for them to finish their little tête-à-tête.

The next thing he'd be inviting Erin to stay for lunch — and expecting her to make it for them! That was not going to happen. She stepped out into the yard and headed for the barn. The company of Rod's men was a million times more preferable.

*　*　*

'Where did you get to?' Gareth asked later.

'I was in the barn,' Rosa replied casually. She would not have him sense she'd been jealous of Erin. 'There was something I needed to talk to the men about.'

'Oh, right . . . ' He accepted her explanation without question. 'I made enough sandwiches for us both,' he said. 'I put yours in the fridge since I didn't know how long you'd be.'

'Thanks,' she said, placated a little. 'I'll have them in a minute. So what did she want?'

Gareth rolled his eyes. 'As usual, nothing in particular.' It came out with a sigh. 'Apparently a friend of hers is having a massive thirtieth birthday celebration in a few weeks' time.' He scratched the back of his neck and paused before adding, 'She wants me to take her there.'

For a moment Rosa had the feeling he'd said yes. Her mouth felt dry as dust. 'You're going?'

'Of course not,' he protested. 'I told her I wasn't interested.'

Rosa couldn't stop herself from smiling.

★ ★ ★

'This is another plus side of the cottage being not far from the beach.' Paul turned to Rosa as she, Chloe, Eva and Nina all walked single-file behind him down one of the narrow tracks running between the sand dunes curving around the bay. 'We don't have to bring the car when we're coming for just an hour or two.'

They soon found a quiet spot that suited them.

'Come on, Daddy,' Eva called the moment they stopped. 'You promised to take us for a paddle.'

'And Aunty Rosa promised us an ice

cream,' Chloe added.

The girls threw themselves down on the sand, and began pulling at their sandals, throwing them aside and squealing when Paul said he'd race them to the distant water.

'Look at them,' Nina said as she and Rosa watched them go. 'You'd think we hadn't been here for years, instead of only yesterday. I can't believe we've been so lucky with the weather.'

'They just love it.' Rosa laughed as she helped Nina smooth out the blanket they'd brought. 'It's a shame you have to go back tomorrow,' she added after they'd sat down to watch the girls and Paul splashing about in the water.

'I know,' Nina sighed. 'I'm bracing myself for a fuss when they realise the holiday's over and we have to go home. Talking of which . . . ' She gave Rosa a questioning look. 'Will you be heading back when all the work here's finished? It's obvious there's something between you and Gareth. There are times when even I can feel the chemistry, but then you seem to withdraw into yourself and he backs off. What's that all about?'

'Obviously your memory is not as long as mine,' Rosa said sharply, feeling defensive. She turned her attention back to the shoreline and in the silence that followed, she knew she had offended her friend.

She turned back to Nina and touched her arm. 'I'm sorry. I didn't mean to sound so bitter.'

Nina gave her a long look. 'I know I'm a tease, Rosa,' she began. 'But joking apart, it's obvious he's crazy about you — and he's a great guy. There's no way you can compare him with Nick.'

The two sat in silence for a while, Rosa finding something interesting in the blanket's blue and yellow pattern and Nina staring out to sea. Around them the excited sounds of children mingled with the cries of herring gulls as they circled around.

'I know he is,' Rosa said at last. 'But

that's what I thought about Nick when we first got together . . . that he was great.'

Nina uttered a sound of frustration. 'He impressed us all at the start. None of us knew how things would turn out.'

Rosa took some reassurance in Nina's admission. 'And there's a kind of ex-girlfriend of Gareth's,' she continued. 'She's always dropping by the farm for some reason or another. She can't keep her hands off him.'

Nina looked surprised. 'Is Gareth seeing her?'

Rosa shook her head. 'Not really . . . oh, I don't know . . . they've known each other since they were kids.' She went on to tell Nina about the few spats she'd had with Erin.

'Sounds charming,' Nina said derisively when she had finished. 'I'm sure Gareth has her figured out. He's what . . . mid-thirties? If he had any feelings for her they'd have been married years ago.'

'Probably,' Rosa accepted, unable to

bear the thought. 'But from what Betsan told me, for the last few years he's had a tough time running the farm. His father wouldn't change with the times and since he died Gareth's been struggling to build it back up again. He hasn't had much time for anything else.'

Nina gave her a dry look. 'You're kidding me! A man will always find time for the right woman. Believe me, you've got it wrong. Where Gareth is concerned, I say just go with what feels right for you. You never know, in a few more weeks you might find you can't stand him after all and wonder why you've put yourself through all this angst.' That devilish gleam was back in her eyes. 'Although I very much doubt it.'

Rosa couldn't help but smile. 'I've never met a man like him,' she said softly.

'Well, there you go.' Nina gave a self-satisfied smile and reached for Rosa's hand and gently squeezed it.

Paul and the girls' return was a distraction.

'Aunty Rosa, can we have our ice creams now?' asked Eva.

'Of course you can,' she said, feeling much happier after opening her heart a little to Nina. She got to her feet. 'But you'd best put your sandals back on. The ground by the kiosk is a bit too stony for bare feet.'

★　★　★

'Bye, Gareth. It's been really nice getting to know you a bit better.' Nina reached up and gave the farmer a friendly peck on the cheek.

'Me too,' he said, giving her a broad smile before doing the same. He shook hands with Paul. 'Hope you'll able to make it back soon.'

'We'll definitely be back for the half-term break,' Paul said. 'Maybe for the odd weekend in between too, if we can manage it.'

'Definitely,' Nina said. She turned to

Rosa and gave her a final hug. 'I'll call you the minute we get back. We'd best get going before the girls start to get restless.' They all glanced across to the car where Chloe and Eva were belted up in their seats looking a little subdued.

Rosa and Gareth waited while Nina and Paul got into their seats then waved them off. Then they stood and watched until the car turned into the lane and disappeared from view.

The farm now seemed so quiet. With their friends gone and the work winding down on the barn, there wasn't the need for the contractors to work the weekends any more.

'Any plans for the rest of the day?' Gareth asked Rosa.

'Nothing special,' she replied. 'I need to move my things back into the cottage. Can I do it now?'

Gareth gave her a look she couldn't translate.

'If you must,' he joked. 'No — seriously,' he added quickly, 'you can come and go as you please. I'll give you a hand if you like — not that I'm eager to be rid of you, of course.'

He paused and glanced away. She was sure she heard him mutter, 'Just the opposite.'

Something in the air almost crackled.

'It's OK,' she said, breaking the gathering silence. 'I'll manage, thanks. There's not that much; just my clothes and a few bits and pieces. Actually I was thinking of driving up to the village later to browse around the antique shop and that little furniture store on the main street. I might see something to suit the holiday lets. I'll let you know how I get on when I get back.'

He nodded. 'I'll be in the fields for a while but I'll see you later.'

* * *

Despite the Easter break coming to an end, the village was still buzzing with people and Rosa was lucky to get the last available space outside the row of shops and directly in front of the furniture store.

She secured her car then crossed the pavement and took a good look in the window at what was on offer before going inside. A set of sofa tables looked a possibility, but she needed to take a closer look.

Inside the rather gloomy interior, furniture was stacked in every available space. At first she thought the shop was unattended until a disembodied voice called from somewhere at the back, 'Let me know if you need any help.'

'Will do,' Rosa replied to someone she couldn't see. She picked her way into the window space. Close up, she liked the tables even more. She reached into her bag for her phone to take a photo of them for Gareth to consider when from the corner of her eye, she caught a brief glimpse of a fair-haired man amongst the crowd of holiday-makers walking in the direction of the shop before he paused and looked away.

The way he had raised his arm and pushed his hand through his hair was almost exactly like the kind of gesture Nick made.

Her instinct for survival kicked in and she desperately glanced around for somewhere to hide. A tall bookcase a little back from the main window display was her refuge. She slipped behind it, all rationality gone, fearful she would hear the shop door open and hear him call her name.

Seconds ticked by but nothing happened. Her hopes began to rise. Maybe she was mistaken after all. While Nina and Paul had been holidaying at the cottage and she had the added security of sleeping in the farmhouse with Gareth merely yards away, she had come to believe what she'd seen in the lane had been her imaginings, pure and simple. Maybe her mind was playing tricks again. Fervently she hoped it was.

She glanced over her shoulder. There was still no sign of the shop owner, but she knew she'd have to move soon.

What would he think if he saw her pressed up against his bookcase?

Her thoughts careered crazily. She was desperate to flee the store, drive back to Gareth and safety . . . but if it was Nick and he was still in the vicinity?

She had to know. She inched slowly forward towards the side of the bookcase. Holding her breath, she took a quick peep at the window display, half-expecting Nick to be standing there, staring into the shop's interior. She expelled a thankful sigh when there was no sign of him, but still she was reluctant to move.

'Seen anything you like?'

Rosa almost hit the ceiling before she turned to see a short elderly man slowly making his way through the cluttered furniture.

His appearance was as haphazard as the arrangement of his goods. His shock of white hair stood on end and the bridge of his glasses was held together by a piece of pink sticking plaster. He peered at her through the thick lenses with some curiosity.

'The sofa tables in the window . . . and this bookcase.' Her words came out in a rush as she tried to overcome the fright he'd just given her. 'But I'll have to bring my . . . ' she stumbled, looking for the right word, 'the person I'm working for to take a look.'

He nodded. 'Anything else?'

Rosa sensed his suspicions about her behaviour but understood. No one looked that closely at a piece of furniture.

'No,' she said. 'Not for the moment, thanks.'

There was nothing else for it, she had to leave. Mentally she straightened her back and headed for the door.

Outside in the sunshine, it took a moment or so for her eyes to adjust to the brightness. Not daring to look in the direction she believed Nick to have taken, she paused for a moment in the shop doorway and focused solely on the car. Bracing herself she hurried over to it, fearing at any moment a hand on her shoulder and a triumphant Nick whispering in her ear, 'Got you.'

Once she was safely inside and the central locking in place, she was still desperate to be gone. Wasting no time, she switched on the engine and pulled out into the traffic.

Mindful of keeping her eyes on the road, Rosa also threw anxious glances at the people milling about on the pavements. Her stomach churned again when just ahead she saw the same familiar figure up ahead, but as the traffic progressed a bus pulled over into an allocated stop and blocked her view. As soon as she overtook it she shot a glance in her rear view mirror to see the man turning into a side street. In that short space of time the momentary image had been reduced considerably, but yet again she recognised the same height, build and the same fair hair.

Her suspicions that Nick was on the island had now became a reality.

Gripping the wheel as though her life

depended on it Rosa increased her speed, eventually leaving the village and the threat she was sure it now contained far behind.

10

The sight of the farmhouse and Gareth's Land Rover parked up at the side of it had never been more welcoming.

With a heightened sense of her own safety, Rosa drove up the track for the cottage and quickly parked up in the yard. She sat there, her hands still glued to the wheel, questions tumbling around in her head but answers beyond her reach.

Had she been right after all when she'd believed she'd seen a figure that night in the lane — and was that figure Nick? Had he caught a glimpse of her just now inside the store, or seen her drive past him in the village? Although he wouldn't know she was driving a different make of car.

But then again, she argued against herself, if it had been him who'd vandalised her car, he'd be aware that by now she'd have a replacement.

Yet if it wasn't him who'd caused the damage . . .

She groaned and lowered her forehead onto her hands, not knowing what to think.

A light tapping on the side window made her jump and she shot back in her seat and glanced up to see Gareth looking in at her, his forehead lined with concern. She got a grip of herself, released the central locking and grabbed her bag.

'Is something wrong?' he asked after she had got out and pressed the fob to secure the car.

Rosa was desperate to tell him what had happened in the village, but she knew what his reaction would be. He would ask if she was certain she'd seen Nick and when she said pretty much ninety-nine percent, that wouldn't be good enough. He might not come right out with it but the thought would hang between them — she still wasn't letting go of the past.

Instead she managed a wry smile. 'No, I just had a near miss with a rabbit. At least I hope it wasn't harmed.' It disturbed her to come up so swiftly and convincingly with such a lie.

He shrugged. 'It's one of the hazards of country life,' he said. 'Don't take it to heart.'

'I'll try not to,' she said.

'How did you get on in the village? You're back sooner than I expected.'

'There were a couple of sofa tables in the furniture store. I was going to take a picture on my phone but — '

She broke off, realising that she was digging herself into a deeper hole.

'But . . . ?' Gareth's gaze was so intense, she had to look away. She focused on opening her bag and dropped her car keys into it.

'I changed my mind about them.' How she hated the lies tripping off her tongue; it felt like betrayal. 'When you have a minute, perhaps we could do some browsing together?'

'One day next week?' he suggested. 'I

can't spare the time to go up there now.'

She nodded eagerly; she had no desire to return so soon. Even with Gareth's company it would be tempting fate. 'Yes, that will suit me.'

'That's settled then,' he said. 'Are you busy this evening?'

'Not particularly. Why?'

'I just thought that a meal at the Ship's Tavern might compensate for Nina and Paul having to go back home.'

Rosa brightened. 'That would be great.' She pushed away the thought that Nick might be in there by telling herself she was becoming paranoid.

'The usual time?' she asked Gareth.

He nodded. 'Sounds good.' Then as he was about to turn to walk away, he added, 'And it might help you forget about that rabbit . . . '

Behind his expression, she couldn't decipher what he was thinking, but there was something in his eyes that told her he had his suspicions and was questioning her explanation.

The moment Rosa walked into the cottage and locked the door behind her, her fears about Nick returned. If the worst came to the worst, could she really handle him on her own?

She had two options. Tonight over dinner, she could tell Gareth the truth about her fears and somehow convince him they were not groundless, or — and she sighed, not welcoming the idea — she could say nothing, carry on as normal and just wait and see how things turned out.

★ ★ ★

'Rosa?' A loud knocking on the back door sent her hurrying through from the living room. 'Damn,' she exclaimed, realising she had forgotten to unlock it before Gareth arrived.

She drew back the bolt and prepared herself to give him some rational explanation. As she expected, his frown demanded as much when she opened the door.

'Sorry,' she said. 'Don't know where my mind is lately. It's probably some subconscious reaction to what happened with my car.'

Would that do? She hoped it would.

His look was sympathetic. 'I expect it will fade eventually,' he said.

Deep down she sighed with relief but it troubled her she was not being honest with him.

'Ready to go yet?' he asked her.

By the time they got there, the pub was busy and Rosa thought they were out of luck for a table, but as they walked up to the bar the owner spotted Gareth and greeted him.

After a brief conversation in Welsh, he turned to her. 'There's a table for us over there.'

She followed his gaze to a far corner. Within the deep recess to the left of the fireplace a table for two had a reserved sign on it.

'I didn't realise you'd booked.'

He bent down slightly and whispered in her ear. 'I didn't, but as the season gets busier Melvyn always keeps a few reserved tables for regulars. He never has a problem filling them.'

After they were settled in their seats he added, 'It's his way of thanking us for giving him the business when things ease off once the holidaymakers return home.'

After they had given their order to a young waitress, Rosa watched Gareth make his way back to the bar for their drinks. The place was buzzing with conversation and laughter and for a moment she envied the other diners' carefree enjoyment.

Stop it! She pulled herself up sharply. She would not let the events of the day spoil her evening.

Determined to enjoy every minute of Gareth's company, she gave him a huge smile when he returned with her glass of white wine and a half pint of beer for himself.

After they'd both taken a sip of their drinks and placed their glasses down, he turned to her, his expression bordering on serious.

'So are you going to tell me the real reason why you locked the kitchen door?'

Rosa was thrown. She'd been sure he'd accepted her explanation. Cheeks burning, she reached for her wineglass as a distraction but his hand enclosed hers.

'Come on, Rosa,' he said softly, 'I know something's not right.'

She met his eyes, knowing beyond a shadow of doubt she was in love with him. 'I wanted this evening with you to be special,' she began huskily, 'with nothing of the past intruding on it.'

He squeezed her hand gently and attempted to raise her mood with a grin.

'C'mon, spit it out. It can't be that shocking.'

Yet at the same time he steeled himself, seeing by the shadowing of her eyes that she was really struggling with something.

She took a long, deep breath. 'I'm

sure I saw Nick in the village today.'
There — she'd said it.

From initial disbelief, Gareth's expression hardened before he opened his mouth to speak.

'Don't say it,' she cut him short. She knew what to expect — a repeat of what he'd said weeks ago.

'What? That you're being neurotic? That you're seeing things?' He shook his head. 'I know you well enough by now to tell when something is really troubling you.'

He squeezed her hand again and gave her an encouraging smile.

'What I was about to say before you interrupted, was that tomorrow we'll call at the store and see Carys. Apart from knowing everybody's business, she knows the ins and outs of every holiday let in the village; when they're booked, who's staying there. He's bound to have called into the store for something since it's the only one that sells virtually everything for miles. You can give her a description and we'll see what she comes up with. Agreed?'

'Agreed,' she echoed, after a slight hesitation. Suddenly she felt a whole lot better.

'Good,' he said. 'It's time we put this behind us once and for all. I don't want you making yourself ill over this, OK?'

'OK.' She nodded, just as the waitress arrived with their order.

Reassured by Gareth's support and suggestion, Rosa tucked into her chicken risotto with the same enthusiasm as he did.

Later after they'd finished eating, and conscious of his working hours, she refused the suggestion of another glass of wine.

'Ready to go, then?' he asked.

'Yes,' she nodded happily.

Although it was getting late the pub was still a hive of activity. A sudden shriek of laughter coming from the other side of the fireplace caught their attention just as they were getting up from the table. She and Gareth exchanged smiles; someone was having a good time.

As they made their way across the crowded room, she noticed the source was a group of women seated around a larger table. Two members of staff were busy clearing it of plates and empty glasses and it was clear to see that much wine had been consumed.

Girls' night out, she reflected. It seemed a very long time since she'd done the same.

They then had to pause suddenly when two of the women pushed back their chairs and got to their feet, blocking the way through. With exaggerated whispers of 'Just paying a visit,' to their friends, they began to giggle their way towards the Ladies'.

As Gareth started to move the chairs back under the table so they could get past, Rosa's heart sank when she caught sight of Erin sitting at the far end. The wine glass she was drinking from looked like it could hold a half bottle. As she went to put down the glass she realised Rosa and Gareth were there.

Rosa saw Erin's expression harden, her eyes narrowing as she stared across at them. She sighed inwardly expecting the usual overblown reaction, but to her surprise, without even acknowledging Gareth, she looked away and joined in the conversation around her, her jarring laughter following them outside.

'Looked like Erin was enjoying herself,' Gareth said as he took hold of Rosa's hand and they strolled back to where he'd parked.

'She did, didn't she? Perhaps you're finally off the hook,' she teased.

'Now wouldn't that be something,' he said with genuine feeling.

* * *

Her first night back in the cottage with a resolution to her worries in sight, Rosa fell into a deep sleep almost as soon as her head touched the pillow.

It wasn't long, however, before she came to with a start when a commotion outside shattered the peace of the night.

She sat up, scared and confused, still half asleep, knowing this time it wasn't her imagination — from around the back she could hear Bryn and Floss barking frantically. The glow coming into her room from the landing window told her the yard lights were on.

Nick . . . he was here?

The thought struck fear into her heart — then she heard Gareth shouting.

Fearful for his safety, she leapt out of bed and pulled her cardigan on over her pyjamas, at the same time struggling to push her feet into her slippers before racing down the stairs.

Out in the yard it took a second to register what she was seeing.

Gareth was struggling to keep hold of a hooded figure who was trying to break free, while the dogs tried their best to defend him.

With adrenalin pumping, Rosa ran over to help, then an almighty yell overcame the dogs' barking as Gareth got the upper hand and spun the person round to face him. He grabbed hold of the hood and yanked it back. Blonde hair fell from its confines.

Expecting it to be Nick, Rosa couldn't believe what she was seeing.

'Erin! What the hell are you doing?'

Bitter anger altered the tone of Gareth's voice as he kept his hold firmly on her arms.

'You idiot!' she raged back at him. 'I was trying not to wake you and then those stupid dogs kicked off. You think they'd know me by now.'

'They do,' he gritted. He commanded the dogs to be quiet. 'But they don't expect to see you alone in the yard at this time of night. What are you doing here?'

'I was driving back from the pub,' she retorted. 'The engine started cutting out, then I saw I was running out of diesel so I thought I'd get some from your emergency supply and tell you about it in the morning. Then all hell broke loose.' She shot a look of fury at the dogs.

Rosa noticed a petrol can lying on the ground and a few rags scattered beside it, not far from where the dogs now sat motionless as statues, tense and alert.

'You know the diesel supply is securely locked,' Gareth said. 'There's no way you could help yourself.'

'Well I forgot,' she defended, challenging him to contradict her.

He looked at her long and hard. 'Let's go and check your tank, shall we, just to make sure?'

For the first time ever, Rosa noticed a flicker of uncertainty in Erin's expression.

'Don't bother,' she spat back, pulling free from his grasp. 'It's up on the top road. Besides,' she threw Rosa a look of contempt, 'I'm sure you've better things to be doing — with your little girlfriend here.'

'It's really no trouble at all,' he insisted. 'I'll walk back with you?'

Erin threw Rosa a final deadly look before storming away.

'Why don't you wait in the house?' Gareth said to Rosa. 'This won't take long.'

She nodded and watched as he hurried Erin around the side of the farmhouse.

Rosa glanced at the discarded fuel can again, then walked over and picked it up, surprised by its weight. She looked at the rags and the possible truth of Erin's intensions began to dawn on her. Shaken, she went inside.

*   *   *

It troubled her to see Gareth looking so pale and drawn when he took the mug of tea she offered him. She followed him over to sit at the table and for a few moments they sipped their drinks in silence.

'She was lying, of course,' he said.

'The petrol can,' Rosa frowned. 'When I picked it up . . . '

'Yes,' he agreed wearily, raking the fingers of one hand through his hair. 'I checked the weight of it, too, before I came in.' He took another drink. 'The day she came round . . . about the party, I didn't tell you at the time, but I told her straight she was wasting her time, that she meant nothing to me; never would.' He shrugged. 'I felt a heel but it had to be said. She brought you into it, of course, so I told her our relationship was none of her business.

'Whatever her intentions were tonight doesn't bear thinking about, but I suspect she was heading for the barn and not thinking about the dogs. Still, one good thing has come out of this night . . . ' His wan smile touched her heart, but before she could say anything, he continued. 'We won't be seeing her again. I've given her an ultimatum that if she ever dares set foot on my land again, I'll go to the police and tell them about tonight and that it was she who damaged your car.'

Rosa was shocked. 'Was it Erin?'

'After what's just happened it hit me that she could have been the one behind it. When I accused her she denied it of course, muttering that all she'd done was try to scare you off with some texts, but I could read guilt all over her face.'

'I can't believe it.' Rosa shook her head, but then recalling that awful day, she remembered seeing Erin's car coming from the direction of the farm when they were returning from having lunch at the Ship's Tavern.

'But I don't understand about the texts. How could she have my mobile number?' she asked Gareth.

'I wondered about that as I was walking back, but then it struck me that she must have got it from the work schedule you gave me for the barn. Remember you used a sheet of your old office stationery? It was probably in full view on the kitchen table along with other paperwork the whole time.'

'Of course . . . ' So the latest and most vitriolic hadn't been from Nick at all. This knowledge brought her intense feelings of relief. 'And you've really frightened her off, then?'

'Oh, yes, I'm quite sure of that.' Gareth spoke emphatically. 'Despite her belief there was no way I could prove anything, I told her if it came to it I'd make sure everyone knew about what went on here tonight . . . the petrol can, the rags . . . and when I added it was bound to affect her father's standing in the community, even on the whole of the island probably since he's made himself that well known, she realised the consequences and her attitude changed.

'Of course as a parting shot she insulted me, my way of life, my family, even the island in general . . . she was returning to London to get her life back.'

He raised his mug and tossed back the last of his tea. 'And cheers to that, I say.'

★   ★   ★

Once more things looked so different in daylight, Rosa thought as she sat alongside Gareth in the Land Rover while he drove up to the village late the following morning.

She knew he was right when he'd said that, despite the incident with Erin, they were still going to get to the bottom of her possible sightings of Nick in the village, hopefully with Carys's help.

As he pulled up outside the convenience store Rosa's mobile rang and when she pulled it out Nina's number was on the screen.

'It's Nina,' she said, surprised to hear from her so soon after yesterday's brief chat to let her know they were home. 'It could be something urgent.'

'Want me to make a start with Carys?'

She touched his arm. 'No, no. I want us to do this together.'

He nodded and remained where he was while she answered the call.

'I just had to ring you,' Nina began. 'I know I said I'd never mention Nick again but I think you need to know this. Brace yourself — this might come as a bit of a shock.' She paused to take a breath before going on. 'Apparently he's been involved in a major fraud and was arrested a few days ago along with several others.'

'What?' Rosa couldn't quite believe what she was hearing.

'Paul's just come back from the newsagent with a copy of today's *Post*. It's splashed all over the front page . . . Local man charged over Peterborough business scam. There's a rather unflattering picture but it's definitely him. Would you like me to read it to you?'

Rosa concentrated as Nina began and, as she took in the details, the names of two brothers who appeared to be running the scam were familiar.

'I've met those two,' she interrupted. 'Think it was last December, a few weeks before I found out about him and Kirsty. We'd called into the Fox and Hounds for a drink after work and they were there. Nick introduced them as old friends.

'I remember them saying they were in the area on business — entrepreneurs they grandly called themselves, but there was something about their manner and their bling I didn't take to at all. You know the type . . . spray-on tan, bleached teeth, full of themselves.

'Nick was more than impressed and eager to do business with them. As far as I was concerned there was no way — I didn't trust them — but it looks like he got into business with them after all.'

'Serves him right,' Nina said with feeling. 'Bail has not been allowed — I think that's because of the amount of money involved — and there's no date for the trial yet as the investigation is still continuing. If you ask me, that man deserves all he gets.'

'That goes without saying,' Rosa agreed. 'I'm glad you let me know, Nina. He was picked up in Peterborough, you said? Well that's cleared up something I've been fretting about for a while.'

'Oh, what's that?'

'It'll keep,' Rosa said. 'I'll call you later and we can talk at length.' She cut the call and turned to Gareth. 'You'll never guess . . . ' she began.

'I've no idea, but judging from your expression, it's got to be something good.'

'Yes!' She smiled. 'It couldn't be better.'

It didn't take long for her to relay to Gareth everything that Nina had said.

'I must have been crazy thinking I was seeing him all the time,' Rosa frowned when she had finished her story. 'But with one thing and another, my head's been all over the place and I guess my imagination got the better of me.'

Gareth reached for her hand and gently squeezed it. 'It's understandable. You've been through a lot and it didn't stop while you've been here — Erin's vindictiveness was unbelievable. I'm sorry for that.'

His apology touched Rosa's heart.

'It wasn't your fault, Gareth.'

'Well, if that's what you think, it's a weight off my mind,' he said. As he held her gaze his expression changed and sent her toes tingling.

'If your head's been spinning mine's been turning somersaults,' he went on. 'Since you arrived on the island, I haven't known whether I'm coming or going.'

They smiled at each other in silence.

'Well, I think Nina's news is cause for celebration, don't you?' Gareth said at last.

'Yes, I do.'

'Fancy a picnic?'

Rosa burst out laughing. That was the last thing she expected to hear.

'Why not?' she agreed. She glanced up at the clear blue sky. 'It's promising to be the perfect day for one.'

'And I know just the place,' he grinned.

* * *

'This is Llanddwyn,' Gareth said after they had walked across a narrow strip of flat golden sand which separated the tiny island from the pine forest behind them. 'Come and take a look,' he smiled, offering his hand to help her up a steep sandy track that curved upwards ahead of them. 'I think you're going to like it.'

A short time later as the path levelled out and they walked on through grassy hillocks, passing by rocky coves and the surrounding sparkling blue sea, Rosa paused for a moment shielding her eyes against the brilliance of a distant white lighthouse exposed in full sun at the southern tip.

'I more than like it. I love it! It's beautiful.'

'There's a cove just a little further on,' he said. 'With a bit of luck we should have it to ourselves.'

Luck was with them and they found just the right spot and spread out the blanket he had produced from the back of the Land Rover.

'I'm starving,' Gareth said as soon as they'd both sat down. He opened his rucksack and began to take out the packets of filled rolls, snacks and fruit and finally the bottled water that they'd bought from Carys's shop.

'Aren't you always?' Rosa laughed. 'Just as well we've enough here to feed an army.'

'We'll see about that,' he challenged, offering her a prawn salad roll.

A short time later, their meal over and everything tidied away, Rosa lay back and basked in the sunshine, wishing their time there could last forever. With her worries over Nick — and Erin, too — finally gone, she had never been happier.

It felt the most natural thing in the world to have Gareth stretched out so close beside her. She loved him with such a strength of feeling she'd never experienced before, it almost scared her.

She wondered if he felt the same way, too. The memory of what he'd said earlier about not knowing whether he was coming or going since they'd met made her smile.

'You're looking pretty pleased with yourself,' he said suddenly. 'Penny for them?'

Rosa opened her eyes and turned her head to see Gareth was now lying on his side, his head propped in one hand, gazing intently at her.

'They're worth more than that,' she said softly.

'Well, I've got prospects and in time I'm sure I'll be able to afford the asking price. Can I give you an IOU until then?'

She pretended to consider what he'd just said at length. 'Hm, I'm not really sure . . . ' she teased. 'Oh, I suppose so . . . ' She began to giggle then suddenly everything changed as his eyes captured hers and she felt herself falling into their beautiful endless depths.

He moved closer and kissed her softly.

'I love you, Rosa,' he murmured.

'Have done from the moment I found you asleep on the sofa and you opened your breathtaking eyes and looked at me. You looked so lost, so defenceless.' His heartfelt sigh lightly ruffled her hair. 'And all I could do was shout at you. Maybe the force of what I was feeling scared the life out of me and it was my way of fighting against it . . . I don't know. One thing's certain, though — whatever your feelings are for me, I'll never stop loving you, Rosa.'

Gareth admitting to being scared? The realisation he could feel just as vulnerable as she was such a revelation it made her eyes glisten with a film of tears.

Smiling softly, she finally pushed her insecurities away as she began to trace the outline of his lips with her finger. 'And I'll never stop loving you, either,' she whispered.

'You won't?' His reaction was almost comical. Grinning broadly he drew her closer still, almost squeezing the life out of her. 'I can't believe it! So you will marry me? You will, won't you?'

'Of course I will,' she gasped. 'That's if you'll allow me to breathe again . . . '

'Sorry!' He quickly eased his hold on her, his concern making her laugh, until he silenced her with kisses.

Eventually they eased apart and he raised his face to the cloudless sky and called out, '*Diolch yn fawr*, St Dwynwen!'

She looked at him with open curiosity. 'You're going to have to tell me what that means.'

Gareth got to his feet and reached for her hands to pull her up to her feet. Slipping his arm around her shoulders he gazed down at her and began to explain. 'I was thanking our patron saint of lovers for bringing me the love of my life. You have your St. Valentine, and we have Dwynwen. And did you know that Llanddwyn is better known as Lovers Island? Dwynwen had a chapel built here over a thousand years ago which eventually became a place of pilgrimage. I'll tell you all about her story later. We have all the time in the world, now — don't we?'

Rosa reached up and kissed him. 'Yes, we do — but we shouldn't waste a moment of it.'

His eyes full of love, Gareth continued to hold her gaze. 'Would you like to see what remains of the chapel?'

Rosa placed her arms around his waist and rested her head against his chest. 'Yes I would,' he heard her murmur. 'Because I need to thank her, too.'

THE END

We do hope that you have enjoyed reading this large print book.

Did you know that all of our titles are available for purchase?

We publish a wide range of high quality large print books including:
Romances, Mysteries, Classics
General Fiction
Non Fiction and Westerns

Special interest titles available in large print are:
The Little Oxford Dictionary
Music Book, Song Book
Hymn Book, Service Book

Also available from us courtesy of Oxford University Press:
Young Readers' Dictionary
(large print edition)
Young Readers' Thesaurus
(large print edition)

For further information or a free brochure, please contact us at:
Ulverscroft Large Print Books Ltd.,
The Green, Bradgate Road, Anstey,
Leicester, LE7 7FU, England.
Tel: (00 44) 0116 236 4325
Fax: (00 44) 0116 234 0205

CALIFORNIA DREAMING

Angela Britnell

When plucky L.A. journalist Christa Reynolds loses her fiancé and her job, she decides it's time for a change of scene. Nearly seventy years ago, her English-born grandmother was evacuated from war-torn London to safety with the Treneague family in Cornwall, and as there's been a standing invitation ever since for the Reynoldses to visit, Christa decides to take them up on it. But she hadn't reckoned on meeting wounded ex-Marine Dan Wilson, and soon she has a life-changing choice to make . . .

SECRET HEARTACHE

Teresa Ashby

Midwife Emma Finch starts work at a new hospital, the Bob, back in her native Yorkshire. It's supposed to be a fresh start for her and her daughter, Keira, but then she discovers that Nick Logan — the man she once loved with all her heart, and who left her when she needed him most — is her department consultant. It soon becomes clear that the old spark between them is still very much alive. Can Emma and Nick reforge a relationship after the heartbreak of the past five years?

THE FIDDLER'S WALTZ

June Davies

In post-war Liverpool, Ellen Butterworth's ambitious sweetheart Brian leaves the Navy and comes ashore so they can begin a future together. An urgent telegram from her younger sister Jeanette interrupts their wedding plans, and Ellen must return to the Yorkshire wool town where she grew up. Unexpectedly, Brian follows her — he wants them to be married there and then in Yorkshire! But, from the moment Jeanette appears in the room, Brian isn't able to take his eyes from her . . .

THE ORCHID

Lucy Oliver

London, 1840: When Ava Miller's father died, she promised she would continue to run The Orchid Theatre and look after its close-knit family of actors. But when Henry Scott-Leigh, the son of the wealthy owner of the theatre, turns up one day threatening to replace Ava or close the unprofitable business altogether, the future looks bleak. Can Ava make a success of the next play and save everything she loves? And what will come of the growing attraction she and Henry share, when they inhabit such different worlds?

TRUST IN ME

Christina Green

Melody Hepworth is made redundant from her job in London, and has parted from her boyfriend. She returns home to the small Devon town where her Aunt Cis runs an antiques business. A lover of vintage clothes, Mel decides to start collecting them again and make a new career, turning the shabby old shop into a sophisticated modern boutique. When she meets attractive local silversmith Rick Martin, there's a spark — but Mel knows she will never trust a man again, let alone allow herself to love him . . .